The Treasure of Juno Moneta

AXEL KAMNE

8TH & ATLAS PUBLISHING

 8TH & ATLAS PUBLISHING

8th & Atlas Publishing
911 Walnut Street
Winston-Salem, NC 27101

www.8thandatlaspublishing.com

This book was ethically and responsibly manufactured by
Lightning Source.

Cover design by Axel Kamne and 8th & Atlas Publishing.
Photo credits: *The Chariot Race* by Alexander von Wagner/Source: Artdaily.com via Wikimedia
Commons. Bronze sestertius of Gaius (Caligula)/Metropolitan Museum of Art via Wikimedia
Commons. Map of the 14 administrative regions of ancient Rome/*G. Droysen's Allgemeiner
Historischer Handatlas*; Public domain via Wikimedia Commons.

print ISBN: 979-8-9919936-0-9
ebook ISBN: 979-8-9919936-1-6

Accursed hunger for gold
— Virgil

THE TREASURE OF
JUNO MONETA

8TH & ATLAS PUBLISHING

1

Green Gnaeus the Great and Greedy held a lottery, and Lucius played it.

Lucius sat at the very top, to avoid the crowds, but the Circus Maximus wasn't fooled by such simple tricks. Despite being the largest arena in Rome, there was never a seat not already occupied by three people and every breath brought with it the stench of a thousand types of sweat. Even Lucius had to plead guilty to the odorous offense. No matter how hard the winter wind bit with its icy fangs, the air was unrelentingly still in the Circus stands. One of many reasons why it was the worst place on Earth.

More by habit than will, Lucius picked some cold, worn quadrans from nearby pockets. The small bronze coins would barely be enough for a day-old loaf, but it made no difference – Lucius was a thief. He felt no shame; it was the only way to survive in Rome. At least, the only way that suited Lucius.

The crowd roared with excitement. It was a chariot race today, just about to begin, and few things were as deafening as the rolling chants of the supporters. But when Green Gnaeus spoke into his cone, they fell into an abrupt silence. Lucius caught every syllable as clearly as if the disgusting little leprechaun spat his venomous words straight into his ear and stirred until the wax ran out, smudging his cheeks. Everyone played Green Gnaeus' lottery. After all, that's what funded the whole show.

By everyone, Lucius really meant *everyone*. Not just humans. Dwarves, blemmyes, even the creatures whose names Lucius went out of his way to forget, were on a constant quest to poverty in their attempts to hit the right number.

"Seventeen, thirty-two, five, sixty-seven…"

Lucius glanced at his lottery ticket, despite being well aware of his numbers, but with a deep desire that he had misremembered. He hadn't. He never misremembered.

He rose instinctively. Forced himself back down to his seat. He would not run, not today. The chariots were in position, and though Lucius hadn't bet on the winner, he would follow the race with great care. The Plan demanded it.

***

Maybe today, if she won, Appia could be free. She inhaled the already dust-heavy air and wished that the race would just begin, that the gates in front of her would open wide. Her horses snorted and scraped their hooves, they sensed it wasn't long now. How Appia had never understood.

Appia turned her eyes to the crowd. There, at the bottom, in the best spot, stood a structure supported by marble columns and adorned with a tiled roof. It was Emperor Caligula's personal box, a secluded room shielded from the crammed benches.

The scrawny Emperor had just risen, and the slaves scattered to not block the view. In his grasp he held a handkerchief, the size of which would've been excessive even for a troll with the flu, and in the cloth, the colors of the four teams were represented: red, green, white, and blue.

The Emperor stood there for a few moments – arm out

straight, holding the end of the handkerchief in his clenched fist – and the whole Circus held its breath in anticipation. Then he opened his hand, spread his fingers wide, and the handkerchief fluttered slowly downward. A gust of wind grabbed it and twirled it in the air before it finally settled on the ground, triggering the starting gates to swing open.

The horses bolted forward. Cheers erupted from the crowd and sand flooded Appias' eyes. Already, an enemy chariot tried to ram her against the *spina*, the bronze-dolphin embellished barrier that outlined the center of the track. A collision with it meant certain death. Appia whipped her opponent's face and he withdrew out of reflex. Good, she went back to whip her horses instead. All four felt energetic.

Curve number one was approaching. Appia leaned to the left, steering through the harness that wrapped around her body. It withstood the strain and she emerged from the curve in fifth place. They were eight drivers today, two from each team.

She took a quick look over her shoulder. Her teammate from the White Team had already crashed and lay buried under his horses. Shipwreck, they called it. The pile of death that became an obstacle on the track.

I've always told you, Appia thought, *don't go too narrow on the first curve*. She was alone now.

She generated a good pace on the straight. Slipped past one in blue whose horses already wearied. Only three left ahead of her. Two red and Hostus, with his beastly black horses.

Second lap. The Reds tried to push Hostus off track, but instead, both of them slammed into the shipwreck. Appia threw herself to the right and managed to dodge disaster. Based on the sounds behind her, not everyone had been as fortunate.

Around her, bits of gravel came pelting from the crowd as they did their best to disturb the remaining competitors. She whipped harder and foam poured from her horses' mouths.

Ahead, Hostus' green clothes fluttered, closer than before – she was gaining on him. Another turn, next lap.

And just like that, she'd reached the race leader.

There he was, the undefeated champion, a porridge-like mess of perspiration and frizzy fair hair. He who utterly dominated the track. Appia needed something special, something extraordinary to beat him.

Still, the crowd was relentless. Their projectiles weren't limited to gravel, whatever they managed to come across was hurled toward the track. From the corner of her eye, she saw something large approaching and made a snap decision.

She dropped her whip and caught the staff. Oak, thick, and heavy.

Most important was the far-left horse, which held the pace and was closest to the *spina* in the curves. Appia rode on Hostus' left side – now, her chance had come.

She slammed her staff right on the muzzle of Hostus' horse. There was a satisfying crack as bones crunched.

Or so it seemed. It was the staff that had actually cracked. The horse shook its head and kept going. *How can it just shake off a blow like that?* Appia thought.

Hostus did not appreciate the attack. He pushed her toward the center, toward the *spina*, and Appia no longer had a whip to protect herself with. She tried defensive maneuvers, she really did, but instead she lost control.

She fell into a massive tumble.

The world now upside down, speed that suddenly felt so much more real. She hung beneath the chariot strapped to the harness, hooves hammering a few feet from her face. A peculiar urge told her to give up, to let herself be dragged along the track and meet her doom. She fought away the thought and used her last strength to reach her waist. The familiar iron of the falx knife against her fingers felt like a blessing from Jupiter himself, and with two swift slashes she broke free and landed after a few rotations as her horses continued in panic.

Appia waited for the charging chariots to pass before dragging herself to safety. Her throat and lungs burned from grit and dust, body aching and screaming in pain.

She watched the rest of the race from the sidelines. Four out of eight riders failed to reach the end. Her teammate was dead, and she wondered if the two Reds would ever be able to race again. The winner's name was bellowed from the same cone that opened the games: Hostus.

Next time, Appia thought – mind numb from fatigue – *next time I'll beat you.*

II

Another day at the Circus, another lottery Lucius played. The numbers had already been announced, but like yesterday, the Plan forced him to stay and watch. He hoped it wouldn't become a new habit. He had enough of those.

The race was replaced with gladiatorial fights, the gladiators brawling in the sand below. Against each other now, the lions were already dead.

"The middle one thinks he'll win, just look how sloppy he holds his sword, but the right one is fifteen times the size. The left guy will just stumble on his unstrapped sandals."

Lucius glanced at the row in front to see who had provided the analysis. A sciapod. He blocked the sun with his hairy foot – two, three times larger than normal feet – and seemed to revel in the shade it cast. Lucius only ran into sciapods every now and then, but the times he did were quite enough, and he rather wished it was more infrequent than frequent.

"Oh stop it, Kezekem," the sciapod's human friend said, "you're not fooling me. No way you see people's sandals from here."

"Yeah-huh *amicus*, I swear," the sciapod said and wiggled his toes. He was terribly pale, and Lucius wondered if it was due to the lack of sunlight. "I never lie, you know that! But forget about the sandals then… you've been having the dotty-chills the past year or what? The big one's Flamma, the half-cyclops – he can't lose."

"Stop already. Doesn't matter what you say, I won't change my bet just so you can make some coins."

Lucius, not without trepidation, had prepared to squeeze further down the seats to make a closer inspection of the gladiators and escape the two's chatter, but now he pricked up his ears. All Circus bets went through Green Gnaeus, such was the law. Break it, and you became the one in the sand.

How dare they talk about it? Lucius thought as they continued their discussion about the bet they'd placed between them. *Don't they know there are Praetorians in the crowd?*

Indeed, already two Praetorians came toward them. They cleared the way by stomping their goat legs and shaking their horned heads. The Praetorians were not only the Emperor's personal bodyguards but also responsible for ensuring that the laws of Rome were obeyed.

When the mass of spectators realized what was about to happen, they did not let the human slip away, fearful as they were of the Praetorians' vengeance; they seized his arms and legs and held him firmly in place, ignoring his shrieks of terror. In fact, they acted so carelessly that the Praetorians, upon arrival, found the job more or less done, settling for a few stomps to spare the poor man further suffering.

The sciapod however, was long gone. An advantage, Lucius supposed, of being the most rapid creature in Rome.

The Circus burst into a unanimous cheer. Down in the sand, one sole fighter towered over the cadavers. One of massive size, heavy armor, and but a single eye. Flamma, the half-cyclops, had been victorious.

***

Lucius remained in his seat long afterwards, pondering. Around him the silence grew as the stands were abandoned. A great number of things had to align for the Plan work, and even then it felt like a gamble. And he hated gambles – that he had Green Gnaeus to thank. In any case, he must tell Pollio, although he had no idea how. If he knew that son of a senator right, he would not only object but scold Lucius for his poor judgment.

When the stands were as good as empty, Lucius left. All he passed were slaves sweeping, a child sobbing with her hands to her face, and finally, the ravens who croaked and squabbled over the remains of that human who thought it wise to circumvent Green Gneaus' rightful share.

Lucius stepped through the gates of the Circus and found himself in the city he both loved and hated. The city that prepared for nightfall, when people were too tired to watch their pockets, when the shadows were easy to hide in, and when he had his last chance to avoid the night shift.

The city lived and slithered – hideous, foul, snaking – an evening like this more than usual.

When games were held at the Circus, all of Rome was emptied – Lucius enjoyed those moments, when he was practically alone in the City of Seven Hills – but now, people once more flooded the streets with their shoving elbows and bad breaths.

He shivered and hastened his steps. Evening came early in the winter, and the cold weather with it. The wind that swept through the streets of Rome never ceased. Luckily, the Circus Maximus wasn't far from Caelian Hill, where many of the finer families resided. When he'd found Pollio's house, a red behemoth of brick, he threw pebbles at the window shutter until Pollio opened. It was a good habit; otherwise, Lucius might go through a lot of trouble for nothing. Ever since the incident with the tree (which had quickly spread in certain circles), Lucius had his reputation tainted and thus preferred the facade path when visiting his friend.

He placed his hands and feet carefully on the marble decorations he'd grown so familiar with and began his ascent. Last time the rain had been so heavy he'd slipped; the fall had been no more than ten feet, but the thump had attracted attention from inside and Pollio's father, Annius Vinicianus, chased him off with a vase.

And the senator had the nerve to say that it was *Lucius* who had a bad influence over Pollio.

"I won't do it," Pollio said as Lucius stuck his head over the window frame.

"Let me at least tell you about it before you say that," Lucius said, pulling himself up the last bit and falling onto the mosaic floor. His arms ached; he was not built for this kind of labor.

"No," Pollio said with folded arms and eyes looking down at Lucius, "it doesn't matter what you say. I'm sick of your ideas."

"Pollio, please!" Lucius exclaimed, did a somersault, and climbed up Pollio's wooden sofa. More precisely, the one whose stylishly chiseled ivory pattern showed Romulus and Remus being suckled by the she-wolf – Pollio had so many sofas that it was best to be specific. "I speak of a job the size that makes your ugly nose look like nothing. The job that ends all jobs, immeasurable rewards."

"And you're gonna throw it all away. Like you always do. Gambling."

Lucius sighed and reached for the grapes in the bronze bowl on a nearby table. Pollio always spoke like that, with questions that weren't questions but statements, and Lucius never knew how to respond. He tried denying everything.

"What," he said between bites. "Never happened."

"No? So you didn't gamble away that bronze statue we stole from the palace last summer? Then where did it go?"

"Too easily recognized. You know we couldn't keep it."

"Or when we stole all the togas from the guests at that fancy bathhouse at Esquiline Hill and *poof* the very same day they were gone."

"Well, yeah, but—"

"Or the hundreds of denarii we snatched from the slave auctioneer last week. In one week Lucius, you gambled away all our earnings in one week."

Actually, that was for something else entirely, Lucius thought, but didn't bother to explain. "Okay, I get it. But no, I will not gamble away our money on the lottery. Not this time, I promise."

"And why would I believe that?"

Lucius rose and placed his hand on Pollio's shoulder. "Because no one will. The lottery will cease to exist."

Pollio blinked with his big brown eyes. His face softened and he finally released his crossed arms. He had understood.

"I know," Lucius said when Pollio opened his mouth. "It's an incredible task to attempt, but by Dis Pater I promise we'll make it. Though we will need help."

"Help?"

"You'll see," Lucius said, walking to the window. Outside, the silhouette of the city loomed in the darkness. Hills rose and fell, and between them, houses and aqueducts huddled in a meandering mess. The evening wind beat against his face; time to go.

"I trust you, my friend. So I trust that you trust me." And Lucius climbed out the window and down the facade.

***

Appia hunched under the whip. It felt different, being whipped by her trainer for losing again compared to her whipping her horses, but she supposed it was the same, really. Ratch-ratch, and her back hurt.

"If you lose the next race like you lost yesterday," her trainer said with a grin that made the boils on his face crack and white pus gently wash over his chins, "you'll stay after the race as fodder for the lions and lizardwolves."

Night had fallen when she left. Appia's team, the Whites, had training facilities and stables on Viminal Hill, so she had to pass the Forum on her way home. The square, which during the day seemed to accommodate all of Rome, was now only populated by a dozen beggars and one or two watchmen-dwarves from the Vigiles who shooed them away. She passed the Temple of Vesta, where the sacred fire always burned, and its flickering light reflected everywhere in the golden statues of the square.

Appia sighed. Every time she saw the busts of the consuls and the generals on their mighty horses, she wished she was as free as them, that she needed not return to her master's house and could vanish in the thick of Rome. But it didn't work like that. Her master would find her. He always found runaway slaves.

Suddenly a man blocked her path, a rather short and slender figure. He resembled a weasel.

"Who are you?" Appia asked, and when she saw his blue tunic, she added, "I have no interest in arguing with supporters."

"Don't worry. I find very little entertainment from the games of the Circus."

He swept a black lock of hair over his forehead – perhaps to cover the wart that he had there – and Appia guessed him to be a few years younger than herself. Whatever that meant, Appia thought she was around twenty, but no one had ever told her when she was born.

"My name is Lucius Turpilinus. I have an offer, something I think would suit you." He awaited her response, but when she stood silent, he pointed with his oddly sore fingers toward Capitoline Hill and the building that stood there as if looking down on the square. "That structure up there, you know what that is?"

"Yeah of course, it's the Temple of Juno Moneta, dedicated to our greatest goddess." She grew annoyed with herself. "What's your point?"

"Well, imagine standing there looking down on Rome and thinking: Wherever I want to go, I'll go, and no one, not even the Emperor, could stop me. Wouldn't that be something?"

Appia frowned. "That's enough. You're just mocking me. *Bonum vesperum.*"

"*Bonum vesperum*, but meet me here same time tomorrow, and you'll win freedom and much more at that."

III

Clemens was by law forbidden to bathe, but he did appreciate that the Emperor held so many of his meetings in the bathhouse. There, nude amid steam and simmering water, it was harder to smuggle in a knife. And as prefect of the Praetorian Guard, it was Clemens' duty to keep the Emperor safe.

The olives Clemens had eaten a couple hours earlier were regurgitated, and Clemens chewed them anew. They were never as good the second time, merely distant memories of the taste remained and the texture was like water.

The man who bathed with the Emperor was a legate, the highest commander in one of Rome's legions and leader of thousands of soldiers on the battlefield. A successful man, with deep furrows in his brow, who'd brought many victories to Rome over the years and who frequented the bathhouse with the Emperor. Wise too, apparently, for he began by chatting about the chariot races and the Emperor's mood turned favorable. In all of Rome, it was known that the Emperor was delighted with the recent triumphs of the Green Team.

Then, when the time was right, the legate presented his matter. "The soldiers' complaints grow louder with each day, Emperor. After they paid for weapons and armor, two hundred twenty-five denarii is not a lot for an entire year's work. Normally

I wouldn't bother the Emperor with such trivialities, but these ever-rising bread prices are causing unrest. Perhaps what's astute is to listen to the masses, assure us of their continued loyalty."

The Emperor sank deeper into his bath, so that even his unnaturally slender neck was hidden by the surface. "How much do you earn?"

"The Emperor is gracious enough to pay me three hundred denarii a week."

"Good. The soldiers can split it then. That should calm them."

"But Emperor!" the legate burst. "*My* wage? How am I to live?"

"You won't," the Emperor said, rising from the bath and revealing his scrawny, complete body. "*Praefectus praetorio*, kill him."

Clemens quickly appeared and yanked the legate out of the bath, splashing water all around. With a firm grip on the man's ankle, Clemens dragged him across the marble floor, neither caring for his floundering struggle nor his desperate cries for mercy.

He stopped a short distance away to await the Emperor, who never missed an execution, and who was hurriedly dried and dressed by a group of slaves. Once the Emperor was ready to watch, Clemens lifted his hooves over the legate's face and stomped repeatedly until only a red puddle remained.

And the olives still tasted of nothing.

IV

They were safe in the underground, Appia told herself. She had – after deciding not to – met Lucius Turpilinus at the Forum earlier and let herself be led down into the catacombs, which had recently begun construction. There, she'd been presented to a certain Pollio ("But call me Annius," he'd said while his eyes made it absolutely clear that she shouldn't), and Lucius asked her to pick a sarcophagus and be seated.

"I'd rather stand," Appia said, demanding an explanation of what it was all about.

Unfortunately, Lucius just raised his hand and said, "Be patient, I'll explain when everyone's arrived."

She crossed her arms and grumbled – her master would be furious when she came home this late ("Relax," Lucius said, "we'll deal with it") – but soon she sat down on the hard, cold coffin and studied her surroundings. Skulls and bones and corpses that only barely rotted – she shuddered – but also peculiar sculptures and rats who cautiously sniffed her toes.

Then came the one they'd been waiting for. He dashed into the tomb so quickly that Appia jumped. No, of course, it was the newcomer who jumped. On one leg. *The Gods*, Appia thought, *it's a shadowfoot.*

"There you are, Kezekem," Lucius said with a wide

smile. "How nice of you to accept my offer."

"I've not accepted, amicus, I'm simply here to listen. So please hurry up and speak before I leave you with the dead and your two-legged friends." He lay down on top of a coffin. The best way to listen, apparently.

Lucius climbed a pile of skeletons to rise above the others. "I've gathered you tonight for something truly special, something that will forever change mankind's – and sciapodkind's," he added, as Kezekem cleared his throat, "view of what is possible. You may have heard of Green Gnaeus' lotteries and bets, the ones allegedly held in honor of Fortuna. You may also have heard that he who correctly predicts the lottery, or can pick every chariot race winner in a year, wins the entire pot. Money amassed over years of gambling at the Circus. Today that figure is seven hundred sixty-three thousand denarii. Well, I say we win them."

"Seven hundred thousand!" Appia exclaimed, having never paid much attention to the lottery, as she needed to make herself and her horses ready for the race. "That much money doesn't even exist."

"I see," Kezekem said. He made a gesture with his foot that made Appia feel like a sculpture. "That's Appia, right? One of the drivers of the Circus? We'll bet on her race, wager she'll be last and trick the leprechaun? A good plan, amicus."

Lucius smirked. "Did I not say we'd win it all? Then betting on the loser won't cut it. Besides, the loser is dead. I haven't known Appia that many hours, so forgive me Appia if I'm mistaken, but I do believe she'd rather not be trampled by some hundred hooves. So no, we will not bet on the horses."

Kezekem scratched his chin with his toes. He had five of them, just like a human, but all were big toes and thick and square and completely wrapped in gray nails. "What then? Play the lottery or what? Nobody wins that, chances are one in ten thousand."

Lucius looked down at his hands and pulled every finger. "Well, let's think... the lottery is between numbers one and ninety-four, six numbers are drawn... first number is one chance in ninety-four, the second one in ninety-three, and hmm... well, of course, the order is irrelevant." He looked up. "That's one chance in eight hundred fourteen million, isn't it?"

Appia gaped at him. *Did he calculate that now?* she thought, terrified. *No, he must be bluffing, right?*

"Oh amicus do get to the point," Kezekem said. "If we neither play the lottery nor the race, how then will we win the leprechaun's denarii?"

Lucius's smirk almost reached the wart on his forehead. "We'll steal 'em."

***

Lucius filled them in with the details of the Plan while feeling pleased that he had already warned Pollio, who never would've approved otherwise. He explained how the Temple of Juno Moneta was teeming with creatures – guarded night and day by countless Praetorians – yet boasted unparalleled beauty. Priests flocked the area, but also coinsmiths, for in nearby houses, all Roman coins were minted and these along with leftover metals were kept in the temple under strict supervision.

Somewhere in there, Green Gnaeus' lottery money also hid, safely tucked away in a place that was already safer than was healthy for a crew of theives.

"Well, who's with me?" Lucius asked when everything was laid out. "Who is willing to rob the temple? This is your only chance to say yes. But, *nota bene*, also your only chance to say no."

Pollio nodded. Kezekem grinned where he lay, giving Lucius the opportunity to scrutinize his thick round teeth from above. They turned to Appia, who'd been sitting silently during the entire explanation of the Plan. Lucius saw the doubt in her eyes, but he would not let her slip away. Not her, who might be the most important of them all.

"I appreciate the offer," she said hesitantly. "Truly, thank you. But it's impossible. My master would notice and punish me. He notices everything. One-twentieth of my winnings is mine to keep; so that I never forget my goal on the track. I only need to win a couple of races, and I can buy my freedom."

"Well, our dear goddess and I offer you more."

"More? I don't need more. I need to win."

Lucius bit off a sliver of nail. The dirt that accompanied it left a bitter taste. He reminded himself to break the habit and said, "I can offer you that too. Let me help you win, just once, and we'll see if you still doubt."

"How would you do that?" Appia asked, looking genuinely curious.

No idea, Lucius thought, but said, "It'll be an easy task, believe me."

Oddly enough, Appia nodded. "When do we start?"

"As soon as we've freed our final member," Lucius replied, and as the other's puzzled looks overwhelmed him, he added, "Did I forget? Our good friend, *soon* good friend, Flamma. You know, the half-cyclopic gladiator? One-eyed? *Big?* Oh stop playing dumb Kezekem! He is imprisoned in the cellar of the Circus Maximus. Only gets fresh air when fighting in the Circus, then straight down to the underground he goes; back to chains and bars. Not those kinds of bars, Kezekem, gods dammit! Apparently not all slaves are as well-behaved as our Appia. Well, it can't be helped, we need our fighter."

V

"I'd like to volunteer as a gladiator, please."

"As a what?" the dwarf from the Vigiles queried.

"As a gladiator," Lucius repeated, while the sight of the real deal made him wish he'd put more effort into his fake beard. "Apparently, this is where they reside."

The watchman shouted at a colleague in the underground, telling him a madman wanted to get locked up.

***

Darkness and filth. The cellars of the Circus Maximus were similar to the catacombs, but instead of the deceased in coffins, there were imminently-deceased in cages.

"What do you flee from?" the new watchman wondered. He was a dwarf, as all Vigiles watchmen were, but with a yellow horsehair plume running side to side on his well-polished helmet. It was the prefect of the watch. Just Lucius' luck, running into the *literal* commander of his soon-to-be enemies. Great.

"Nothing. Simply felt like becoming a gladiator, that's all."

The prefect grunted and Lucius followed him deeper into the cellar. Torches flickered faintly from the walls, and as they walked, the insults trumpeted from prisoners who caught sight of their jailer.

"Everyone flees from something. But if it's glory you seek, you've come to the wrong place. We have nothing but murderers here. Murderers and arsonists. There's no better way to condemn people to death than by the Circus. They ain't got no glory, these scum. There is nothing glorious in being a gladiator."

Lucius flinched as a lion threw itself against a cage they passed. It roared and bared its teeth, shaking its thick mane.

The prefect smacked the lion with the flat side of his sword and laughed raucously. "We have beasts as well. But don't worry. The bars are forged out of black eel iron. They're indestructible."

They moved on. The dwarf waddled forward, his wide shoulders and round belly forming a body far heavier than Lucius', and counting the plume, Lucius couldn't even enjoy being the tall one for once.

"How come Vigiles are guarding a place like this?" Lucius asked. "I know dwarves like being underground, but isn't this beneath you proud firefighters?"

"You don't think we'd rather hunt salamanders if we could? That's what we used to do, before the Emperor came to power. Impaled salamanders with spears and feasted. They roast themselves, you know, those scoundrels; they've got no protection from their own heat when they're dead. But the Emperor won't let us touch them, it's like he wants the city to burn."

"I see. Well, I can help you with that."

"Help?"

"Yes, I can overthrow the Emperor for you."

The prefect spat. "I was wrong. You don't flee – you really are mad."

***

Appia readied the chariot. A larger model than usual, one that could carry them all. It hadn't been easy getting it out of the stable without her trainer noticing, but at least she didn't have to drive. She was far too well known around the Circus, so Lucius had deemed it safest that she sat in the back this time. And besides, they had planned something special.

"I don't get our leader, amici," Kezekem said as Appia handed him the harness. "We'll rob that temple, sure, but then is it really so smart to first free a gladiator? And before we free the gladiator, we must also free the leader himself? Sounds like a worse mess of soup than that I had from that cook… What was his name, *pe-something*? Yeah, that guy who always made ivory meals."

"Just wait," Pollio said. "Lucius knows what he's doing."

***

"You bastard of Orcus!" the prefect yelled, slapping Lucius with the back of his hand. Lucius' cheek burned, and he had no time to recover before getting shoved into a grimy cell.

"No please! Don't leave me here!"

"Play with Flamma, he's a killer of twelve souls. I'm sure you'll have fun together."

Wow, you really are sensitive, Lucius thought as the bars slammed shut, a loud clink of the locks following. *But it's true, that plume does make you look like a rooster.*

And so, Lucius was alone with Flamma. The latter occupied nearly the entire cell, despite sitting cross-legged on the ground in an attempt to be as small as possible. Up close, Flamma was even more fearsome than when he fought in the Circus, despite the lack of armor.

He glared at Lucius with his plate-sized yellow eye, no longer covered by a helmet, and said with his wide mouth, "Dwarf here? I *hate* dwarves."

"I'm no dwarf," Lucius replied, already starting to regret stomping grapes with a murderer, "even if I happen to be shorter than you. Most people kind of are."

"Yes," Flamma said, pointing at Lucius' chin. "You dwarf."

"A mere disguise, I promise." Lucius pulled off his beard. It felt good to escape the itchiness.

Flamma's sole eyebrow formed into a *V*. "Disguise. Why?"

They were interrupted by the return of the prefect. "You made me forget something, scum." There was a rattle as he searched for the right key to the lock.

Did the rooster have to come back? Lucius thought. If he showed himself without a beard, the prefect would know something was wrong – not even the Vigiles were that stupid – and he couldn't really scratch it back on without getting caught.

"What is it?" Lucius asked, with his back to the prefect.

"Nothing of note. An oath to swear. You'll have to come up to the Circus, that's where we swear in the newcomers to get them in the right mood."

"You're dead if you come in," Lucius said sharply.

Behind him, Lucius heard the prefect chuckle. "You think I'm afraid of you? You will be a gladiator, it's too late to change your mind." And the lock snapped as if being unlocked.

"No, nobody is afraid of me, but you should be afraid of the half-cyclops. Flamma was just telling me how much he hates dwarves. How he longs to rip out the heart of a dwarf and chew it into pieces."

"I see." It clicked again, locking once more. "Of course, you might as well be sworn in right here in the cell. The Circus is empty of visitors in this late hour, anyway. Repeat after me…"

"I swear," Lucius said, "to endure to be burned, to be bound, to be beaten, to be killed by the sword."

The prefect hurried away, leaving Lucius and Flamma in the dungeon.

VI

"Well, where were we?" Lucius said when the prefect was out of earshot. "Oh right – I was just about to help you flee."

"Flee?"

"Yeah, everyone flees from something, apparently. So crack open the bars here."

Flamma rose and bent head and spine to not bang into the crumbling ceiling. "Crack bars? You mad. Black eel iron – four human fingers thick. One half-cyclops finger thick."

"I'm just a little mad, I think. But considering how many called me that recently, maybe I'm wrong." Lucius stuck his hand inside his tunic, fingers burning as they clasped the icy but familiar shape. "This is the Jadecrystal," he said, holding the stone toward the half-cyclops, who squinted in an attempt to discern the deep dark green little gem in the dim light of the underground. "It contains an ancient Egyptian power, granting extraordinary strength."

"That? Normal stone. Only gods give strength."

"Don't be so boring. Just try it. You'll find its magical powers more than sufficient."

"In that case – you use it."

Lucius rubbed his face. *This was harder than expected*, he thought. "I'm too weak for the power. You, on the other hand, are strong enough to survive. That is, if you dare."

A set of hulking thumps sounded as Flamma beat his chest. "Course dare. I Flamma!"

"Right," Lucius said and handed over the Jadecrystal. "Close your fist around it. Do you feel the power surging through your veins? Do you feel it?"

"I feel! I feel! I invincible!"

"Use it! Break the bars! Set yourself free!"

With a roar that made the ground shake, Flamma slammed his fist into the bars, making pieces of black eel iron fly in all directions.

Lucius allowed himself a leap of joy from the cell. "I told you, my dear Flamma, I told you! Follow me, to freedom!"

Flamma remained standing with his arms crossed on the other side of the broken bars. "Don't want to."

"You don't want to?" *Oh the Gods, I thought we were done with the persuasion.*

"Yes – want," Flamma explained. "Only with Brontes."

"Brontes? We haven't got time to save more gladiators."

"Brontes no gladiator," Flamma said, after which he did something peculiar. He formed his lips to an *O* and blew out a shrill note; a cheerful whistle that poorly fit the situation.

Then she came running – no, *slithering*. She had paws, but these somehow moved sideways, a face like a reptile with a long forked tongue, and the tail as a serpent itself, her back covered in scales. A lizardwolf.

She scurried to Flamma, made little leaps and licked his knees.

Lucius shuddered. He enjoyed seeing what the gods could create, but it was something else entirely to see their work so *close*. "By Dis Pater, are you friends with these beasts?"

"No," Flamma said. "Only Brontes."

And so, they fled at last. They sprinted through the

tunnel, while gladiators in other cells gaped, astonished or apathetic.

The Vigiles were already en route to meet them. They must have heard Flamma's roar, or − Lucius thought with amusement − his whistle. When they saw the lizardwolf they recoiled by reflex.

"After me," Lucius called, running into a side passage that he knew led out from the cellar and to the backside of the Circus. It was a steep climb, and although Lucius was so tired that he constantly slipped in the mud, they pulled away from the pursuer's short legs. Then the faint starlight appeared before them. Exit, freedom...

Blocked by a dwarf. A well-armed dwarf wearing a helmet with a yellow plume: the prefect. Apparently, he wasn't such a coward as his earlier behavior had led Lucius to believe. He stood firmly, not twitching a muscle, and held out his sword, called gladius − which was very much relative to him in size − ready to thrust and twist.

Flamma tackled him. Attacked with elbows and punches to the dwarf's head, like hammering a nail. The dwarf managed to twist his sword and Flamma grunted and bled from his gut. A couple more punches, and the dwarf was knocked out.

They continued. It couldn't have been more than thirty strides left but Flamma was moving ever more sluggishly. The cries of the pursuers grew louder. *They will stop us*, Lucius realized. *They will stop us, and I really will be burned and be killed by the sword.*

It was at that moment, that he felt something slithering between his feet. The lizardwolf turned back to the guards. She stepped in their path and growled and hissed. And Lucius and Flamma were out in the fresh air of the night.

The chariot stood ready, and strapped in front of it was Kezekem, his face so crestfallen that Lucius almost regretted forcing the sciapod to serve as a draught animal.

Pollio helped them into the chariot. "How'd it go?"

"You see that, don't you?" Lucius said in between gasps that reminded him of his hatred of sprinting. "We're free."

The chariot rocked as Flamma got on, and it became so cramped that Lucius ended up in the half-cyclops' lap. That was something Lucius would've preferred to avoid, for Flamma's gaping wound leaked so much blood that Lucius would need to steal a new tunic.

"Ready amici?" Kezekem said. "Hold on tight."

"No," Flamma replied, but before the others had a chance to ask what was wrong, the lizardwolf jumped up the chariot, landing in what surely was meant to be Flamma's lap, but instead became Lucius'.

When the Vigiles also appeared, Kezekem didn't ask a second time. He bolted off and the wheels spun up dirt. The world became blurry in the trail of speed, and though Kezekem naturally must have moved by jumping, the chariot neither shook nor trembled.

"Sorry," Flamma said, and to his surprise Lucius noticed how the gladiator's eye shifted in color from blazing yellow to murky indigo. "Must turn back. Lost it."

"Mhm," Lucius mumbled, carefully shoving the lizardwolf away as she whipped out her slimy – *venomous* – tongue and licked his arms. Only then did he realize what Flamma had said. "Lost *what?*"

"Jadecrystal," Flamma admitted. "Magical. Ancient Egyptian power. Gone."

Lucius shuddered – the lizardwolf really did have disgusting scales. "Oh," he said, "don't worry. It's nothing but a normal stone. Forgive me, but all you needed was a boost of confidence."

VII

Clemens was summoned to the Emperor. Not summoned to guard duty, but *summoned*. Clemens hadn't the faintest idea what he'd done wrong, but surely it was something, for he could feel the trouble all the way down to his hooves.

Gates opened, closed; alone with an Emperor on a throne.

"You have a new task, *praefectus praetorio*," the Emperor said with his usual blank stare.

Clemens nodded slightly. Hopefully, the new task wasn't being thrown to the lions.

It wasn't. But pretty close, all things considered. "My most bloodthirsty gladiator, a giant, or cyclops, or whatever he is, has been freed from the cellars of the Circus Maximus. You must find these thieves that stole him from me."

Stole a gladiator? That sounded like pure madness. "But Emperor—"

"Jupiter," the Emperor corrected. "I am Jupiter, King of Gods, Lord of Thunder, Ruler of the Skies. So call me that!"

"Alright, Jupiter, but isn't this a task better suited for the Vigiles? The Praetorians have more important things to handle. Like guarding Your… Godliness."

"Those fools lost him in the first place! Why are you still

here? Go on! Off with you, stinking animal!"

***

The dwarf glared up at him. "Why are you here, Praetorian?"

Does everyone have to ask that? Clemens thought and said, "If you must know, it's to rectify your mistakes. And it's by order of the Emperor, so you'd better let me through."

The dwarf snorted, but let Clemens down to investigate the scene of the crime. Clemens questioned the watchmen he met, but everyone said the same thing: that it was no concern of him, that they didn't snoop around the Praetorians' business, that he could take his goat hooves and stomp 'em up his ass. Clemens truly felt like informing them that belonging to the Emperor's bodyguard wasn't exactly something he desired, that fauns captured by Roman troops didn't have a *choice*, but it hardly would've helped.

Finally, he found a dwarf with a black and blue face and dried blood in his beard. The commander of the Vigiles, *praefectus vigilum*. His helmet was dented and dirty, but the plume was yellow, and he was in the midst of polishing his armor.

"Your watchmen are not of the helpful kind," Clemens said, "but perhaps you can tell me what really happened here last night?"

"Do you recognize me, Marcus?" the prefect asked with an oddly lisping voice. "We met three years ago. Oh? You don't recall? It was at the Emperor's feast, the one where we celebrated that his headache was gone, or as he said, that he'd returned from the dead. You weren't a prefect then, but I remember how you stood there, laughing, like everyone else. No, sorry, not like everyone else. Louder, more violent. I noticed you then, and I've followed your journey through the ranks ever since, keeping a safe distance."

"Laugh? Why did we laugh?" In all honesty, Clemens didn't remember much from the occasion. He had drunk one – three, five, twelve – cups of wine that night.

The prefect grinned, showing his seemingly freshly made teeth gaps. That explained the lisping. "The Emperor's men sewed me into a thick leather sack together with an adder, a monkey, and a rooster, and then threw us all in a barrel of boiling water. I don't know if the worst part was the ever-rising water, burning everything it reached, the monkey's scream, or the rooster's frantic pecking of my body in the dark, but the adder bit open the seam and I was able to tear myself free. Do you understand? Punished by *poena cullei* for having done nothing wrong. I, who'd served Rome faithfully and been *praefectus vigilum* for ten years, was publicly humiliated for no reason but the Emperor's entertainment. I thought I was on the right side of the law, that I was judging rather than being judged, but there are no rules around the Emperor."

Clemens remembered now, a little. "I'm sorry we got such a bad start, mister…"

"Thrakatulus."

"Mister Thrakatulus. But I hope we can leave the past behind. We must cooperate, prefect with prefect, and do what is best for Rome."

Thrakatulus reached his eye, the right one. Pressed it to stop it from twitching. "I'll help you, but on one condition: that you send those scum to me when you find them."

***

A young man had volunteered as a gladiator, and though it sounded mad Thrakatulus had believed him; the man had worn a fake beard, a sign, Thrakatulus noted, that he fled from something. Then, he'd been thrown into Flamma's cell, and they'd escaped together with a lizardwolf in a chariot dragged by – no, the prefect wasn't joking – a shadowfoot. Apart from the fake beard, the thief had black, curly hair and a wart on his forehead so large that it might not have even been real either.

Such brute strength, Clemens thought as he studied the smashed bars, and suddenly, Thrakatulus' injuries seemed more justified. *But why all this trouble for a gladiator?* Clemens had heard of Flamma; indeed, he'd even seen him once, defeating fourteen giant Indian gold-digging ants without much trouble, but it was something else entirely to stand right in the havoc he'd caused.

Clemens was done with the Circus. Apparently, the chariot the prisoners escaped in resembled those used in races, and he decided to visit the stables of the teams to see if they were missing anything.

On his way out of the cell, he felt something under his hooves. Something that clung on and refused to let go. After repeatedly shaking his leg to no avail, he gave up and leaned down to pick it off.

What a curious stone, he thought, examining his finding. It was perfectly smooth, without the slightest bulge, and of a deep dark green color. It could belong to one of the watchmen, or the stolen gladiator himself, but its beaming shininess led Clemens to believe it was far more expensive than any of them could afford. The thief's, perhaps?

Clemens slipped the stone into his pocket. The stables weren't the only place he planned to visit.

VIII

Appia had gotten used to the catacombs, she had to admit. The darkness and the silence provided a strange sense of security. She wasn't even worried of the wrath of her master – he who owned her and let her compete in races as an investment. No, not anymore. Last night he'd caught her sneaking back to her sleeping place but had only given her a brief glance, before returning to his work in the sooty light of a tallow candle. Appia didn't understand how, but somehow Lucius had kept his promise and "dealt with it."

Now they had other things to deal with.

"I'm counting with four weeks," Lucius informed the crew. All had gathered, except Flamma, who was so badly injured that he needed to rest. "Four weeks before the Vigiles find us."

"Find us?" Kezekem said. "Nah, why would they?"

"For if I know the Emperor, he'll be furious over his loss of Flamma. He will order the Vigiles to search every inch of this great city, and their commander knows my face."

Pollio cleared his throat.

"What?" Lucius said, and Appia couldn't tell whether his irritation stemmed from being interrupted or from not being interrupted.

"So, I've asked around; heard from my contacts," Pollio said.

"Good, that is why we have you."

"And the Praetorian prefect, Marcus Clemens, was summoned to the Emperor yesterday. They spoke in private, after which the prefect paid a visit to the cellars of the Circus Maximus."

Lucius bit his nails. Then he continued toward his knuckles. The rats drew near, emboldened by the silence.

"The Praetorians guard the Temple of Juno Moneta and the Praetorians hunt us... well, it seems the goddesses of fate spun our threads for us to meet. That bit I said about four weeks – we'll change it to four days."

Four days! Sure, Appia understood that the Praetorians were more dangerous than the Vigiles, but four days! Until recently she'd lived her life as she always did, risking her life at the Circus, never having heard of any Lucius Turpilinus. Now she would rob a temple. It felt absurd.

Lucius must've sensed something in her face, for he turned to her and said, "Do not think I've forgotten my promise. This puts greater pressure on all of us, but I will still help you get that race win you desire."

Oh yeah, the race. It was set for the day after tomorrow. Appia tried to convince herself that it was unimportant, that it didn't matter if she won or lost, but she had fought for a victory all her life; because she had been whipped and because it was her chance to be free. The robbery gave her a much better chance, but it was a *different* chance.

"Thank you," she said, nodding.

Lucius moved on. "Pollio, keep listening to your contacts. Discreetly of course, the usual methods. The Emperor might very well become the key to our operation. Find out about his plans and the senators' attitudes. And we must keep an eye on this Clemens… Kezekem?"

"Huh?" the shadowfoot said. He crushed a flea with his fingers and flicked the corpse through the air. Appia saw more climbing up his nose. They too seemed to be holding council.

"You like the shade, don't you? Well, I want you to shadow Clemens. Follow his every step and never let him out of sight. He will not say as much as *culpam poena premit comes* without you noticing."

"Sure, sure, that's a pretty long phrase anyway. What will you do, amicus?"

"I will take care of the wounded. Flamma is still struggling from the wounds inflicted by the Vigiles' commander. He'll need a few days to recover."

"A few days," Pollio interjected, "not four I hope."

"I'll ensure it isn't. The die is cast, on the ninth day before the *kalends of Februarius*, we rob the temple."

***

Lucius had told the truth, he would take care of Flamma. The half-cyclops rested in an insula Lucius rented in Suburra, the neighborhood where you took three steps and got robbed five times. It was, of course, a pleasant challenge to steal back what had been stolen, but sometimes Lucius wished he could live as well as Pollio did. Well, there were benefits with Suburra too, like being able to drop off a wounded half-cyclops in the middle of the night without awkward questions from the neighbors. And in four days, Flamma needed not only to stand on his legs, but also live up to his role as a fighter.

But first Lucius had to explore the temple. There was still so much they didn't know, that wasn't possible to know, that they needed to know.

Dragging steps up the steep slopes of Capitoline Hill,

passing temple after temple marking the hill as the home of the gods, to the *Arx*, the walled summit of the hill, and so it rose at last: the Temple of Juno Moneta, in all its glory, glittering in Apollo's evening rays. The building was supported by white marble columns surrounding it on all sides, chiseled with such grace that the temple despite its humble size still was the most beautiful temple in Rome.

Today's ritual was just finished. A priest stood there, at the altar outside the temple, next to him a flutist and a broad-shouldered *victimarius* with an axe hanging loosely in one hand. On the altar, red of blood, lay the head of a white bull calf sacrificed in honor of the goddess.

The priest said a few words, and the crowds scattered. The flutist disappeared with them, the *victimarius* took care of the bull head, and the priest cleaned the altar. Lucius took the chance.

He was stopped at the gate, the massive double doors of bronze. Four Praetorians stood on guard, their mouths working in constant rumination.

"Where do you think you're going?" one of them asked between bites, whipping his tail in the air.

"Me?" Lucius said in a not quite successful attempt to act surprised. "I'm just visiting the temple."

"The ceremony's outside – and it's finished for the day. Go to another temple or come back tomorrow."

"The statue," Lucius tried, "of Juno Moneta and her geese, it's in there, right? All my life it's been a dream to see our greatest goddess with my own eyes."

"Are human ears really that bad?" the Praetorian said, stepping closer to Lucius. "You're leaving. I don't like to repeat myself."

Lucius backed away and stumbled over the man who suddenly stood there, wrapped in a toga. It happened to be the priest.

"Pay no attention to the Praetorians," he said, helping Lucius steady himself, "we can permit a simple worshiper. Follow me, I'll show you. She is magnificent, our Moneta."

The Praetorian grunted as they went through the gate, and when Lucius stuck out his tongue at him, his noises evolved into bitter curses.

It wasn't the first time Lucius visited the temple, but inside it was more crowded than he remembered. Metal and other scraps piled up in every corner, and when a coinsmith with his arms full of denarii angrily pushed his way past, Lucius quickly made the weekly salary of a baker. Maybe he should've known better than risking everything for a few coins, but despite it being more Praetorians in one place than Lucius thought possible, and the whole temple shook with the slam of their hooves against the stone floor, no one noticed Lucius' little theft.

"Here she is," the priest said as they reached the far end of the temple.

Juno Moneta was built by a true master. Her posture was imposing, standing with a staff in one hand and the other on her waist. Her hair was tied up and adorned with laurel leaves, and her draping clothes seemed so light, despite being made of the finest marble like all the rest and painted with the utmost artistic care. At her feet were two geese: one frozen mid flap, upright and with unfolded wings, the other sitting hunched, eyes staring back at Lucius.

"She's beautiful," Lucius said, not only in an attempt to maintain his image as a devoted worshiper.

"Her name derives from warning," the priest said, apparently interpreting Lucius' words as an invitation to lecture. "Four hundred years ago, during the Gaulish sack of Rome, the invaders tried to sneak up Capitoline Hill in a daring plan to surprise the valiant defenders. Then, in the darkest hour, Juno

Moneta ordered her sacred geese to honk, and the defenders were warned. They held out until the army arrived, and Rome lived on. We owe it all to her – imagine, we would've been Gauls otherwise!"

"Mhm," Lucius mumbled, while he caught a glimpse of how the *victimarius* – the sacrificial slaughterer – left his axe in the storeroom and headed to a corner of the temple, carrying a sack dripping with blood. There he stooped and knocked on the floor. To his surprise, Lucius saw a trapdoor open and the *victimarius* descending into the underground.

Five knocks, Lucius thought.

"And the Gaul tossed his sword on the scale and said—"

"What do you do with the leftovers?" Lucius interrupted.

"Leftovers?"

"Yes, the animal consumption in a place like this must be something else. And no one gets a taste out there; you always get a bite of what wasn't burned for the gods at the rites, but never here, I've noticed. Never at the Temple of Juno Moneta. Strange, isn't it? One might wonder where all the meat goes?"

The priest's eyes grew dark. "So that's what you are? A maggot begging for food. Be very careful how you address me, or you'll discover soon enough that Moneta has stopped watching over both you and your coins. Did you want to hear about the statue or not?"

"My apologies," Lucius said, after which he endured the priest's complete discourse on the subject.

IX

"No," the alchemist said, examining the stone more closely through his strange lens, "it's no emerald... where did you get it?"

"If it's not an emerald," Clemens said, ignoring the question, "what is it?"

The alchemist mumbled, stroking his kelp and seagrass beard, which splayed over his entire face, barely leaving space for anything but his eyes. (Which, fittingly, glittered like gemstones.)

"Oh? Nothing special... might as well get rid of it. I'll help you, sure, twenty quadrans for your trouble, since you came all this way."

Clemens shook his head. He hated being in the alchemist's shanty – it was filled with odors impossible to place – but he wouldn't leave without an answer.

"Forty then?" the alchemist continued. "No? Fine, one full denarius!"

"It's not for sale."

The alchemist shifted position and interweaved his fingers. "Now that I really think about it, it occurs to me that it might have some sort of low, tiny, petty value after all. But it's difficult to say how much. Here's the deal: you'll leave it here for analysis, and return in a few days when I can give you a better estimate."

Clemens grabbed the alchemist's beard – an easy thing to grab – and lifted him in the air. "You think I'm an onocentaur? Never try to fool me, Chymes! Tell me everything you know, or I'll send the entire Guard to take care of you. They would enjoy it, every single one of them. Believe me."

"Fine, fine, just let me down!"

Clemens let go, and the alchemist landed on the earthen floor with a thump.

"Yeah, I admit," the alchemist said, rubbing his beard. "It's made of jade. A very precious gemstone. Highly valuable."

"Good, anything else?"

"No…"

A kick. Ah, how soft the alchemist's belly felt around Clemens' hooves.

The alchemist squealed. "Yes, fine, I'll tell you everything! It's the Jadecrystal! The ancient stone used by the old Egyptians to build their three thousand-year-old lasting Empire!"

***

When the alchemist had calmed down, he revealed everything he knew about the crystal: that it was a legend among his brethren, desired by all but believed by few, that its composition was unknown, but that theories ranged from sulfurized mermaid tears to hardened lynx piss, and – most importantly – that its powers were of such a monstrous nature that the possibilities appeared endless.

"Yes," he continued, his excitement quickly fading the memory of both his own unwillingness to help and of Clemens' threats, "it was no coincidence that the pyramids were built in Egypt. Take the Great Pyramid of Giza *ad exemplum*: the base is 440 by 440 royal Egyptian cubits, and the height is exactly

280. If you multiply these by each other – like the Babylonians did – you get 123,200 cubits. Take that times two and you get 246,400, multiply that by ten and you have 2,464,000. And do you know what is 2,499,035 cubits long, and thus only differs with 35,035 cubits in length, the mysterious number thirty-five twice? Naturally, the distance between the great pyramid and Babylon! Sounds reasonable?"

Before Clemens could answer, the alchemist continued. "Naturally not, as a Babylonian cubit is shorter than an Egyptian cubit. The Egyptian measure is longer with a factor of 737 over 51,860, and if you use that instead, the distance is exactly 2,464,000! A sign from above, the Jadecrystal called to the Babylonians, revealing its position at the Great Pyramid of Giza!"

"What do the Babylonians have to do with anything?" Clemens said, feeling more than a bit confused.

"Nothing. Nothing and everything! It's no longer a secret that the Babylonians, and especially King Esarhaddon, were familiar with the movements of the planets... they calculated the distance to the sun as 284 billion Babylonian cubits, which naturally is 332 billion normal Roman cubits, that is 99 million Roman miles. So what, you ask? I'll tell you, in royal Egyptian cubits that's 280 billion – precisely one billion times the height of the pyramid!"

"How do you know all this?" Clemens asked, who, admittedly, had heard a thing or two about Chymes' wisdom, but still found himself surprised by the man's vast knowledge of things that hardly could be a part of everyday alchemical life.

"How I know?" For a moment, the alchemist seemed unsure, as if he didn't know what to say – perhaps he ran out of air – but then he caught his breath. "It's common knowledge, even the slaves know this. Did you think it was a coincidence? That King Esarhaddon was so learned in astronomy, and that it was he who finally crushed Egypt? Naturally not. He had personally interpreted the movements of the stars, and felt the Jadecrystal calling to him from the darkness of the Great Pyramid. That's why he invaded Egypt. But when Esarhaddon grew mad and perished, the Jadecrystal was passed on to his son... yes, to Shamash-shum-ukin, naturally. Ashurbanipal got the kingdom but Shamash-shum-ukin was the eldest, so the crystal must've gone to him. So it stayed in Babylon a few more years, after which its movements are unknown... but that reminds me! How did *you* get it?"

***

Clemens left with the Jadecrystal in a tight grip. He didn't trust Chymes – and hadn't understood half of what the alchemist actually had said – but he didn't think the alchemist dared lie any more.

What if it's true, he thought, glancing at the stone without loosening his grip. *What if this green little thing both built the Egyptian Empire, and brought it down.*

He shook his head and horns. The story seemed incredible, but it was probably best not to think too much about it. Couldn't be good for one's health. The answer to the real question was still just as far away, the Gladiator Thieves were still cloaked in darkness. All that remained was to investigate the race stables.

Since he happened to be on Viminal Hill, the stables of the Whites were closest. It wasn't long before he knocked on their gate.

"By Neptune stop kno—" The trainer's face appeared behind the door hatch. It was hideous. "Aha, a Praetorian visiting this late hour. Do come in, I guess."

Inside, it smelled of hay and horse, a pungent and musty

attack on the nose. *How come it never smells like roses*, Clemens thought gloomily.

"What's it about?" the trainer asked, after he shooed away two drivers and some stable boys.

"Just an inspection," Clemens said, eyeing the poorly hidden red backs of the drivers. "There was a theft the other night, and the thieves fled in a racing chariot."

"I've got nothing to do with it."

"Nobody said you did. But perhaps you're missing something?"

The trainer ran his hand over his boil-ridden face. "No, no, not at all. Everything's here. But, um, yes. You might want to check out Hostus."

They were interrupted by a terrible ruckus further into the stable. A horse neighed and stomped its hooves and kicked its legs. Other horses joined, and Clemens was reminded of how stupid and noisy horses were. Not in any way like goats.

"Who's there?" the trainer shouted. "Oh, it's you," he added, as a young woman appeared by the horse. "Get lost!"

Clemens glanced at the woman. She had thick hair tied behind her neck, and eyes resembling mountains rising from the sea. Another driver, it seemed.

Poor thing, he thought, *living like this*. Clemens didn't blame her. Likely, eavesdropping was the only fun she had. The chariot races must be the opposite.

"Yeah, Hostus then," the trainer said again, "the star driver of the Greens. There's something fishy about him."

Clemens said goodbye. It was obvious that the trainer accused this Hostus in order to get rid of the competition, but perhaps it was still worthwhile to visit the driver.

***

Appia followed the Praetorian out with her eyes, thanking all the gods that she and Pollio had gotten the chariot back safely last night without any trouble. Cautiously, she made her way back to the trainer.

"What was that all about?"

"What? You're still here? I told you to get lost, or I'll get the whip again! And what it was about is no concern of yours."

X

Insulae – the rickety buildings that plagued all of Rome had gotten their names from how the streets flowed around them like rivers round an island. The first time Lucius had rented an insula, he'd been happy to get a room on the top floor. There you had a better view, and you were less likely to get someone's excrement dropped on your head.

It quickly became apparent that his joy had been a mistake.

The lack of headroom didn't bother Lucius much – he was spared from the wry neck that the sporadic visitor immediately suffered from – but he hated the vermin. Thornlarvas, wingless flies, cockroaches – all climbed upwards. Every step was accompanied by the crunch of their bodies, and those hanging from the ceiling fell on his face when he tried to sleep.

Lucius had only lived in the insula a few weeks before it burned down. (A salamander attack; it was said that the fire hadn't been particularly severe, but one seventh of the city had burned that night – it just happened to be the seventh that nobody cared about.) His second insula had been absolutely indistinguishable from his first. Perhaps it didn't smell as bad, but Lucius suspected that was due to the thin walls giving him a cold.

After three unusually calm and peaceful days, his second insula collapsed. The fat senator who owned it cheered over the fact that he could build a new one and demand a higher rent.

So it continued – fire, fire, collapse, collapse, fire – and Lucius kept stepping on cockroaches on the top floor.

It was to his current insula, a colossus of mudbrick, that Lucius was headed; he crossed the courtyard, dodging rooting pigs and muddy children chasing ducks. Inside, there were several rooms, but as usual, Lucius passed them in order to climb the staircase that ran centrally through the building. Despite covering his nose, he couldn't escape the stench of pig. At night, the animals were brought in to live together with the tenants.

On the top floor, two doors faced each other. Lucius opened one of them.

The mattress that Flamma was lying on had been squashed by his weight, and reeds were sticking up around his figure as if they were growing at the edge of a lake. Very well, it was far too small for him anyway.

"I wasn't really sure what half-cyclopes eat," Lucius said apologetically, handing over a sack of mutton and sheep's milk.

Flamma grunted, and sat up halfway. The bandage Lucius had applied was red. As Flamma dug into the food, the lizardwolf slithered closer, her forked tongue hanging halfway out of her mouth. Flamma threw some meat to the animal, and Lucius kept his distance.

"Your beast isn't much of a guard dog," Lucius said. "She only emerges when dinner's about."

"We alike. Brontes and I," Flamma replied, as grease dripped from his lips and down his chin. "Brontes loves food. More than anything."

This statement, however, quickly proved flawed, as Brontes dropped her piece of meat, rushed up to Lucius and gleefully licked the denarii Lucius had stolen in the Temple of Juno Moneta. Lucius, suddenly struck by an irrepressible sense of generosity, quickly emptied his pockets, letting the lizardwolf peacefully cover her new possessions in mucus.

"And shiny things," Flamma added. "She also loves."

"I should go," Lucius said, carefully taking a few steps from the lizardwolf, fearing further assaults. "You… both of you, seem to be doing fine on your own."

Flamma blinked a couple of times, his eye changing from yellow to brown. "You think we're animals. Not just Brontes. Me, too. Monsters."

"No, Flamma, no…"

"Maybe so," Flamma continued. "Maybe I'm monster. Killed cinnamon merchants. Twelve of them. Smashed skulls with fists. But you should know – good reason."

"What happened?" Lucius said, instantly regretting his words. He was not in the mood to listen. (He never was, really.)

"Sit," Flamma prompted.

Lucius declined the invitation – he didn't want to get any closer to the vermin than necessary – but Flamma still began his story.

"Raised in Syrian desert, close to Palmyra. Barren world: hot, relentless. Beautiful. Mountain ranges over horizon. Golden brown sand like lovely rug. Only tufts of grass push up. Alone. And animals. Antelopes with horns longer than legs, cut like saws. Through all – except Euphrates' trees. Beavers with sixteen teeth. Eagles soar high. Eyes so strong they stare at sun. Not blinking, not missing. Dipsas – terrible venomous snakes. You see them, already trod on them. Feel bite, already dead. Pards, spotty and swift. Camels, stupid – only drink brown water. But humps bigger than backs, and eyes in tail. Jaculus, feathered serpent. Throws itself between treetops. Turtles with strong shells. Heavy stone against it, knock knock, they unharmed. But in summer rain they crack. And, of course, majestic, magnificent, wonderful, holy – *T'rrch'un*."

"Trr... what?"

Flamma got something wet in his eye. A tear perhaps, but it was the size of a denarius. "Cinnamon birds, you call them. Huge. Red tails, descendants of Phoenix. Builds nests of cinnamon sticks. High. Few trees can handle size. Cinnamon merchants want nests. To crumble. Make spice. They climb up – but birds peck hands. Fall. Break every dirty bone."

"Good," Lucius said to please the half-cyclops.

"Yes. But cinnamon merchants don't stop. By African traders – imports live elephants. Slaughter animals. Cut them. Big bloody chunks. They throw meat at ground. Cinnamon birds dive, snatch meat. Take to nest. Weight makes nest fall to ground. Then, path clear for merchants. Seizes cinnamon."

Flamma stopped for a moment, his eye shimmering red. "What happens then? You know? Birds' eggs in thousand pieces! That's why I'm gladiator. That's why I'm murder. Saw twelve merchants. Cinnamon in hands."

Lucius felt obliged to say something. "I..." he started.

It knocked on the door.

Knocked! Hard, determined thumps. Why would anyone knock on their door? No one should knock on the door! Lucius hadn't even heard any footsteps.

He signaled to Flamma to be quiet, who had already grabbed Brontes' jaws to keep the animal still. Carefully, Lucius crept over to the small window, and opened the shutter. He pushed his way out, feet first, a few steps down the wall, a jump, and landed on his butt, splashing mud over the courtyard. A pig bumped him with its snout.

Lucius pushed the pig away, entered the building, and tiptoed up the stairs. Indeed, there was someone at his door. Someone with only one leg.

By Dis Pater, what's Kezekem doing here!

Lucius went up to scold him. "What are you doing? You mustn't come here, *ever*! We don't want to draw any attention. And didn't I tell you to shadow Clemens!"

"That is what I'm doing," the sciapod whispered, his skin even paler than usual. "Clemens is on his way here."

XI

The Gardens of Lucullus was the most exotic place in Rome. Crammed with opulent buildings, baths, paintings, sculptures, fishponds, and – of course – plants, it made even the Emperor's palace look like nothing but a pale shadow in comparison. After the death of Lucullus almost one hundred years ago, it had quickly passed through the hands of those among the Roman elite who could afford its upkeep, before, finally, being purchased by its current owner, Valerius Asiaticus.

The purchase had been a scandal. Asiaticus was a blemmye – he had no head, having his face on his body instead – and since he was of Gaulish origins, he wasn't considered a true Roman; but that was soon forgotten when Asiaticus first became a senator, and then became their leader by being appointed consul.

As far as Lucius was concerned, it made no difference who happened to own the garden, as long as he could have a bite of what it had to offer. *One shouldn't let the gifts of nature go to waste*, he thought as he munched on a nicked lemon. It tasted sour, but at least not as sour as the citron he'd picked the day before, which had caused his mouth to erupt in fierce protests.

He passed the famous cherry tree, casting longing looks at its bare twigs – it was not yet the season for cherries. The tree was Rome's first, long ago imported from the Black sea provinces, and despite countless efforts over the years to make it spread, no other cherry trees had sprouted from the Roman soil.

It had been only a few weeks since Lucius had arrived in Rome, alone in the city the world revolved around, but it hadn't been long before he'd understood what he needed to do in his new life.

As an evening routine, after making his living in the most crowded streets of the city, he often went to the gardens to visit the magnificent library that was located there. Every time he asked the stiff old scholars if he might read a few papyrus scrolls, perhaps on philosophy, mathematics, law, or ecology, and the scholars always snorted at his request, pointing out that the unique collection of the library was for members of the noble families, not dirty street urchins who barely reached the shelf.

Very well, at least the question made him feel more honest when he snatched the texts in front of their dim eyes.

Tonight, he'd gotten his hands on two scrolls, which he eagerly read as he sat in the secret room he'd found in the darkness of the library. One dealt with mathematical problems, but he quickly got bored with it, since he constantly had to dip his reed pen in more ink to correct all the errors and flaws he found. The second was more interesting: a bestiary, listing all types of beasts, and their terrible powers.

Fauns, he read, slowly and with great difficulty, in the light of a candle, *often referred to as goatmen. Lower body like goats, legs exceptionally powerful, tail gives good balance. Upper body similar to humans, but with better blood circulation. Head with pointy ears, and very sturdy horns. Descendant of the sacred woodpecker Picus, son of Saturn. Originally from the wild forests east of Rhenus; captured in the campaigns of Emperor Augustus, and by his divine might transformed into the most glorious warriors of Rome, the imperial Praetorians.*

A detailed illustration below the ornate letters showed a faun in gleaming armor and red cloak. The resemblance to the Praetorians he'd seen patrolling the city streets was striking.

He continued in the scroll. The next beast had no text and the illustration was more vague. Just some kind of gray mass with lines in all directions. Lucius followed the rough lines with his fingers, leading to a lump in the center of the beast. He wrinkled his nose. There was something eerie with the image.

He shook his head. It wasn't to learn about beasts that he'd gone to the library on this particular day, it concerned that odd incident that had happened yesterday. During Lucius' regular stroll at the Forum, a merchant had asked him to take a look at his goods – and by goods, he meant a green little stone.

"Why?" Lucius asked, yet still approaching the merchant. There was something alluring about him, his red robe and his flat, mustachioed face had a certain aura of mystery.

"It brings good luck, little boy," the merchant said with an accent Lucius had never heard before.

"Good luck?" That sounded useful.

"Or bad luck. Or no luck. I don't remember. It's probably not important. Yes, perhaps false, perhaps true. Lightning, clouds, it has a mind of its own. An Egyptian crystal of pure jade."

The only thing Lucius knew about Egypt, was that the Queen who once ruled it, had a nose so large that it obscured the rest of the face. But the merchant's nose was the opposite. An impostor, surely.

"You are not Egyptian! And not Roman either, I can tell by your clothes!"

The merchant smiled. "Who said I was? I have traveled far and wide in this world, searching for the most marvelous objects, and now, I am selling the most powerful to you alone.

Here, in the heart of Rome."

It was, of course, nothing but a load of rubbish – that Lucius had understood right away – but the stone was so beautiful that he hadn't been able to suppress the impulse to spend the coins he'd earned from the pockets of the square.

If only I found some scroll on geology, he thought, eyeing yesterday's purchase, *or at least on Egypt. Anything that would help me understand.*

A creakingly crack sounded behind him. By instinct, Lucius drew the stone toward him. The two scrolls fell to the floor.

"Who are you, that dare defile my personal chamber?"

Wearing the most magnificent toga Lucis had ever seen, shining white with purple stripes, a blemmye entered the dark room. The toga was cut at the front, revealing a face: hard, black eyes across the chest, pointed, knifelike nose below, thin, stretched mouth over the belly. Lucius often saw blemmyes in the streets, where they played silly games and made fart noises at passing noblemen, but it was clear that this blemmye possessed an utterly different kind of dignity.

Lucius grew cold when he realized who it was. "Oh, no, no, please, mister, please. I didn't know…"

"And you've doodled!" Valerius Asiaticus bellowed as he saw the mathematics scroll. He picked it up and waved it in front of Lucius. "Do you have any idea how expensive these scrolls are?"

"I… no, no… sorry, but it was wrong."

Asiaticus stopped and stared at the scroll. After a while, he raised his eyebrows toward his collarbones and muttered, "Hmm, perhaps. Still, that's no excuse for breaking in. Just wait until your family hears of this. Who's your father? A senator?"

Lucius looked at the floor. He tried to push away the images of the day it happened. The day the Roman soldiers had arrived. "I... have none. None at all, no family."

Asiaticus studied the scroll again. Most blemmyes walked with hunched backs and slumped shoulders, but Asiaticus had a proud posture that, despite the lack of head, made him look taller than many large men. He seemed to make a decision. "Don't worry. You can stay here tonight."

"In the library?"

"In my villa. The slaves will arrange a bed for you. I'll take care of you, for now. There is a thing or two you ought to learn."

Maybe it's true, Lucius thought, loosening his clutching grip of the stone. *Maybe it does bring luck, after all.*

XII

Clemens had found them. Lucius didn't understand how, but there wasn't any time to figure it out. And it was impossible to escape – Kezekem had said that Clemens wasn't far off, and, regardless, Lucius wouldn't leave Flamma in the lurch.

They snuck back into Lucius' insula. Flamma had risen from the squashed mattress and stood with his back bent in order to fit. He wobbled and held a hand to his belly, but his fists were clenched, ready to fight. Footsteps sounded from the stairs. Not regular footsteps. Precise, heavier thuds – hoofsteps.

And so he had come, the enemy, Clemens. He who could stop it all. Lucius couldn't help himself, he pushed the door ajar and peered through the gap.

Clemens stood with his back turned, showing his cloak and his thick fur that stuck up between the armor. He opened the opposite door.

Huh? Lucius thought. *He lives here?*

Lucius, of course, didn't keep very good track of his neighbors – impossible when moving so often – but he was still surprised to find the Praetorian prefect living in such a place. He'd always assumed that the Praetorians, as the Emperor's bodyguards, were paid handsomely.

Clemens must've heard something, for he turned

around. A face with horns, goatee, and two fiery red eyes stared back at Lucius.

Caught. Well, he couldn't just stand there like a spy. Lucius swept a lock of hair over his forehead, opened and closed his door, nodded to Clemens and said, "*Salve*." Whereupon he went down the stairs in rhythm to his pounding heartbeats.

Clemens returned the greeting and went into his room.

***

Ratch-ratch, and her back hurt.

And so, yet again, Appia was on her way back to her master. Through the streets of Rome. In windy winter darkness. Tomorrow it would happen, the race. The first since she met Lucius and his companions. The first where she would get *help*. How, she didn't know. Had they bribed drivers? Sabotaged chariots? Tampered with the horse gates? Upon question, Lucius had simply switched the subject, but she had little choice but to trust him. It felt wrong to cheat, but Appia supposed that was a feeling she needed to get used to. She would rob a temple, after all.

Her master's house was on Caelian Hill, built as was befitting for a senator like him. Appia sneaked in – a new habit, already well established – despite not needing to since she actually returned from her training at the right time.

That's why she heard them speak.

The noises came from a door – the kind that always was closed, and that Appia had understood that she never should open. She didn't do that now, either, but she did put her ear against it and listened.

Eavesdropping like a criminal. Was she a criminal yet? Soon a robber.

"He's worse than ever." Appia recognized the low, severe

voice as belonging to her master. "What can anyone do against such madness?"

"There is one thing we can do," another voice replied, sounding strangely similar to her master's.

Silence. Then her master spoke again. "If we try that, Uncle, we'll be equally mad. The Emperor is beyond reach."

"Perhaps he isn't. Yesterday I was approached by a stranger. A peculiar man. Peculiar dress, peculiar accent – but he was very persuasive. We're not alone in this. The stranger mentioned several interesting names."

Appia felt a hand on her shoulder. She spun around – already, in her thought, cursing herself for getting sneaked up on during her own sneaking – and found herself face to face with Pollio.

"Pollio!" she hissed. "What are you doing here?"

"I'm listening," he whispered, putting his finger to his mouth.

"Good names," her master continued from the other side of the door, "but I'm actually surprised you're not mentioning ex-consul Valerius Asiaticus. In all of Rome, no one hates the Emperor more than he does. Not since what the Emperor did to his wife."

"Perhaps we should be glad that he didn't get the question. It's wise to have powerful friends, Nephew, but never as powerful as Valerius Asiaticus. Six years ago, who would've guessed that a blemmye would become consul? It should be impossible – Jupiter, it *is* impossible – but Asiaticus became one anyway. We cannot have dealings with a person like that, neither as friend nor enemy. I fear the temptation would be far too great for him once it's all over. And we can't afford that, can we?"

They chuckled slightly, and the conversation died. Steps approached the door.

"Quick!" Pollio said. Unnecessary advice, of course; she

was faster than him up the stairs and around the corner. They peered down to the door that was just opening.

"Goodbye then, Uncle," her master said.

"*Bonum vesperum.*"

The visitor left, and Appia's master turned his head. He looked straight at her.

No surprise, no anger, just eyes that met hers and felt like the whip on her face. Then, he saw Pollio – who breathed down her neck – and his gaze turned to iron.

"Annius! What are you doing, my son? Come down at once. I've told you, do not associate with slaves."

XIII

Clemens was at the chariot race. The one thing, next to gladiatorial fights, that he loathed the most in the entire world. Pure savagery, unnecessary competition and unnecessary death. It reminded him of the Capture.

The rest of Rome was there, too. Shouting, eating, sleeping. The usual mix of high and low. Clemens sat not far from the Emperor's box, but he wasn't there as a bodyguard – today, he would scout.

The leprechaun, with his green clothes and flame-colored beard, read the numbers. The lottery had almost become more popular than the races, but Clemens didn't find it much better.

The Emperor threw his handkerchief.

The drivers whipped their horses. Rode the first curve, second curve, back where they started. First lap done. A lone driver in a white cloak pulled away from the rest.

Will you look at that, Clemens thought as he recognized the woman who'd eavesdropped on his inquiry with the boil-ridden trainer. *Seems your trainer's methods are paying off.*

She was on her way to victory. Her opponents swarmed behind her, attacking each other in such a way that they – despite merely having suffered one crash – couldn't possibly catch up with the leader.

That's what Clemens thought, anyway, but a green driver decided to demonstrate how little Clemens actually knew about the sport. Hostus – for it must've been the driver Clemens had been warned about – rode through the storm of enemy whips, breaking free from the pack with his black horses.

One lap to go, white still in the lead. Supporters shouted, "Appia! Appia!" Perhaps she was blinded by the cheers, perhaps she pushed the horses too hard, for suddenly, Hostus was right next to her.

The cheers were replaced by the Greens. "Hostus! Hostus!" And even aimed at one of his horses. "Incitatus! Incitatus!"

On the home stretch, Hostus overtook her and won.

***

Appia was so angry at having lost, that she forgot to think about the fact that her master was Pollio's father. Or, rather, she lost because she'd only thought about just that.

And because she hadn't gotten any help. Lucius hadn't done a thing. Had he even been there? He had *promised*.

What did you expect? she thought, annoyed with herself. *That he'd jump down in front of the horses and stop them with a calculation?*

But he had promised. Just like he'd promised they'd rob the Temple of Juno Moneta. It would never work.

He waited outside the Circus. Even though she'd changed into regular clothes, and huddled with tens of thousands others leaving the Circus the same way, he caught sight of her and waved eagerly. Perhaps it was because Pollio stood next to him; apparently, good eyesight was something of a family trait. She didn't want to approach them, but she did anyway.

"That went well, didn't it?" Lucius said with a smirk,

although he seemed slightly worried about all the people around them.

"Went well? We lost. No, *I* lost – you weren't there!"

"I mean well as in you not falling off the chariot and getting run over. That would've put a spoke in our wheel, if you'll pardon the expression."

Appia didn't feel like pardoning Lucius for anything.

"You need not worry," Lucius continued, "our sciapod is shadowing the enemy. Clemens still has no clue what's going on."

"Like me, then? Who is also kept from all the secrets? When were you, for instance, going to tell me that my master is Pollio's father?"

At that, Pollio turned to the color of a greek strawberry. The kind that, if thrown into a potion, had no purpose other than taste.

"Oh?" Lucius said, glancing between the two. "That is known now? Yes, I was wondering how long it would remain a secret. To be perfectly honest, I was surprised that you didn't recognize each other right away. Well, of course Pollio did, but not you. You didn't recognize him. I suppose your training at the stable has taken too much of your life for you to keep track of everyone running around at Vinicianus' house. Perhaps it's time to reveal the rest then too. Hmm, that is why it wasn't important that you won today."

And Appia actually thought he seemed… embarrassed? Some sort of hesitation, at least.

"I made a deal with your master," he said, his eyes focused everywhere but at her. "Well, not *I* didn't obviously. Annius Vinicianus isn't very fond of me. I asked a friend for help – he likes to dress up – and through him I bought you, under the condition that you could continue to live in his house."

Appia felt but a mere emptiness. "How… when?"

Lucius' eyes were steadier now. "From the beginning, I'm afraid. A part of the Plan. The Gods know you weren't cheap, several hundred denarii. To not gamble them away…" He shook his head. "Dis, it's my biggest accomplishment yet. But it was necessary to buy you, there was a risk you wouldn't say yes."

"And then you would've forced me? Forced me to rob a temple, I who am your slave?"

"Honestly, what do you think, Appia? Of course you aren't my slave. It was only intended as a bribe. An unnecessary bribe, it turned out. You are free."

Appia couldn't take it any longer. Couldn't talk, couldn't see Lucius or Pollio anymore. She ran.

Behind her, she heard Lucius' voice. "Appia, wait! You have to! It must be you! Jupiter…"

Appia ignored him. Why would she keep trusting him, the way he'd lied? Why would she do anything at all? She was free.

Free.

***

Clemens hurried his steps. Hostus returned to the stable by himself, his horses led by someone else, and Clemens wouldn't let him slip away. Not he who had won again, despite being behind and facing attacks from his opponents. No one was that good, not even at something as meaningless as riding. Something was wrong, and Clemens would find out what that something was before Hostus met anyone else.

And the driver actually seemed to act suspiciously. With each step he took, he glanced behind his back, as if sensing that he was being followed, but without noticing the follower. Clemens knew his kind; so preoccupied with his own thoughts, so preoccupied with flight, that every backward glance was merely a part of the process, something automatic, not understanding what his eyes saw.

What a doofus, Clemens thought with amusement, given how his own figure had to stand out in the Roman mass of people.

Finally, Hostus turned into a side street. The evening had already begun, and the street quickly grew empty of witnesses. Seemed like a good opportunity.

Hostus jumped when Clemens put a hand on his shoulder, and when he turned around, Clemens got a chance to look at his face. A disappointment. Hostus' hair was very curly, but fair instead of black, and there certainly wasn't any gross wart on his forehead. It wasn't the man who'd freed the gladiator.

Fine, but there had to be more than one.

Clemens slammed Hostus against the wall, hissing – well aware of the effect his appearance had on humans, "Admit it! Admit that you participated in stealing the gladiator!"

Hostus' eyes grew wide; lips moving without the smallest sound being heard.

"Is that how you win your races too? Drawing power from the Jadecrystal? Admit it! Admit it all!"

The driver broke down. "Y-yes, I admit," he sobbed. "With a saw. I did it with a saw."

"A saw?" Clemens said. That wasn't right; the gladiator hadn't been sawed to freedom. "What d'you mean?"

"The h-horn, I sawed it off with a saw. My beautiful Incitatus! He suffered as I did it, his eyes told me. And all j-just to win! How could I sink so low? Oh, h-how could I believe anyone would take a unicorn for a horse!"

A unicorn? By Saturn himself!

"Please, don't tell the Emperor!" Hostus continued, his cheeks snotty and red. "He'd persecute me for all eternity!

Imagine, I sawed off the only h-horn of h-h... I sawed off the only horn of his beloved horse!"

Yes, that would certainly mean death. Lying about the Emperor's favorite horse – not telling him it actually was his favorite unicorn – and wounding it so badly at that. But it sounded like a useful secret to know. In any case, Clemens doubted such a coward could've been involved in the Gladiator Theft.

"I won't tell," Clemens promised, "provided you're willing to help me."

XIV

Six years earlier

Lucius hated being in the midst of a crowd. It reminded him of what he had to do before Asiaticus took him under his wing. His life as a thief was over, and he went to extra lengths to stay away from the Forum. Particularly during the day, when the square was at its busiest, and *especially* when big events were held. But he hadn't much of a choice, now. He needed help.

The six Vestals – dressed in long, white *stolae* that fully covered their gracile bodies, fluttering in the wind like the togas of some of the high-class spectators – stood in front of the Temple of Vesta as smoke billowed up behind them. Rome celebrated Vestalia, the annual festival in Vesta's honor, and during a few days, the temple, normally forbidden territory for all but its guardians, was open to the public.

Spectators sang praises to the goddess, while the Vestals hung flowers around a donkey's neck, thanking it for chasing away Priapus in the well-known legend. Inside the walls of the temple, the sacred fire of Vesta still burned. As long as the fire lasted, Vesta protected the city, and never in eight hundred years had it died. Not from storms, not by drunk Vigiles watchmen, not by anything. It was as eternal as Rome. Vesta did not abandon them.

Concluding the ritual, the Vestals danced around the donkey, whistling happy tones as the gates of the temple were thrown open. A ruckus arose when the mothers, who'd gathered to make offerings in hope to get their family blessed, all decided to be the first one to enter the temple. Lucius took a deep breath and elbowed his way through scents of mashed pears, aged cheese, and garlic-spiced turnips; someone spilled thick wine in his hair and it immediately became sticky. He too lugged a sack over his shoulder, bigger than himself and as heavy as Ajax' shield, but it didn't contain any food.

Despite his trouble, Lucius had to wait quite a while inside the temple. He watched the sacred fire, burning in the middle of the temple with ferocious, crackling flames. The smoke stung his nose before slowly drifting up through the hole in the ceiling. Finally, a Vestal was ready to see him. The right one.

"Take off your shoes, *puer*," the Vestal said sternly with a soft voice, leading the way to a secluded room. "Only the humble deserve Vesta's blessing."

"Sorry, Sacred Vestal," Lucius peeped, taking courage, "but I'm not here to be blessed."

The Vestal frowned. "Why then, have you come?"

Lucius glanced around to make sure they were alone. Then he spoke quickly and without hesitation, as Pollio had instructed him when they'd practiced. "I have a friend whose hobby is knowing things that no one should know. He gave me the idea, and I beg you, predict my future!"

"Who do you take me for? I'm a Vestal. I do not engage in such things. Ask an augur; he might study some crows' flight patterns for you, if you pay him well."

"That's not good enough. It has to be an absolutely certain omen, the kind you only get from studying a dead animal's liver. Yes, I've heard of your haruspexian methods."

The Vestal snorted. "You make it sound so dramatic. It's nothing strange among priests. My vows don't forbid me."

"Right, they only forbid that you… that you…"

The Vestal looked at him with one eyebrow raised, and Lucius felt a blush burn his face.

"Your vows only forbid that you break your chastity," he said hastily. "Or worse, let the fire die out. But it's Vestalia now, as you may have noticed?"

The Vestal stood silent, her six braids sprouting from her head like twigs from an olive tree.

"Well, then I don't think people will appreciate that you, a sacred Vestal, are killing donkeys in your spare time. They, who are to be revered and honored; imagine if it were to be known. Remind me, what is the punishment for a Vestal who fails Rome? Oh, I know! Buried alive!"

The Vestal showcased her impressive jaw muscles by gritting her teeth in what must've been rather close to the breaking point – and for a moment, Lucius was sure he'd end his days thrown on the sacred fire – but then she cursed at last. "Priapus, but they have the best liver! Alright, *quid pro quo*, what kind of omen do you want?"

Lucius dumped the sack at her feet. It felt good to be rid of it.

"It started shortly after I arrived in Rome," he blurted while the Vestal pulled the donkey out of the sack. "I didn't want to, but I played on Green Gnaeus' lottery. Played, and played again, and now, it's like a part of me. And a few days ago, I had an epiphany. Fortuna herself revealed which number would win."

He stopped himself by slamming his jaws in a way that wasn't comparable to the recent display of the Vestal, but was enough to make his teeth shake. "But it was wrong! You see?

Fortuna tricked me. And now I owe silver to people you don't want to owe a button. That's why I need an omen. I just want to make everything right. Please, please, you have to help me."

The Vestal tore up the donkey's skin with her bare hands. "Whatever," she muttered. "Alright, this is fresh, killed just one or two hours ago, good, good. Hmm, the liver is glossy and nicely filled, that indicates a strong omen, and the gallbladder is shaped like a fasces." She stuck her head down and took a deep breath. "The bile is sour but the blood smells heavily of iron, interesting. And a touch of hay, as well. Her last meal, I suppose.

"Yeah, well that's that," the Vestal said, looking up. She wiped her red, slender fingers with a white piece of cloth. "You will receive help from the Circus. Jupiter's chosen will come to the rescue. In the darkest hour, she will save all of you."

"All of us?"

"Do not interrupt. No one will be as quick, no one will shine as bright. Jupiter's chosen, she will save you."

"But the lottery!" Lucius grabbed her arm. It was colder than ice. "Don't you see? I need to win, or I'm done for! And you speak only of some Jupiter's chosen!"

The Vestal's eyes widened, her braids quivered and rose; they took the form of something wild, open mouth, fangs, tongue sticking straight out – snakes. Lucius shied away as his cheeks grew numb.

"Do not touch me, you minion of Priapus!" she bellowed, her voice suddenly deep. "You know what you must, get out of my temple!"

***

Lucius tried to shake off the unpleasant feeling on his way home. He hated snakes, how they slithered, the texture of their scales, and even more so when they comprised part of someone's hair.

And now, apparently, the Vestals were gorgons.

He wished it meant that the omen was a lie, but if anything, it just made it more true. How typical, help of Jupiter's chosen. It should make him feel special, he supposed, but in the end, he wasn't a single step closer to winning the lottery. And in a few days, the thugs would demand their loan back.

The summer heat was just kicking in, for the first time painfully demonstrating to Lucius how hot the city could be. By the time that Lucius – who first had to climb both up and down Quirinal Hill – found himself on the right hill and saw the Gardens of Lucullus rising in full glory, he was drenched in sweat and starving to get inside. True to his habit, he glanced at the cherry tree as he passed; a few fruits were cautiously picking their way on its twigs, but they weren't yet red. It could still be weeks, Asiaticus had said.

Lucius nodded to a librarian, and continued deeper into the library in search of his mentor. A slave hurried toward him.

"No lesson for you tonight, Lucius. The master wishes to see you in his *tablinum*."

Odd, Lucius thought as he let himself be led through all the corridors and rooms that formed the vast building complex, *he never lets me skip my lessons*. Not that Lucius complained about that. Yesterday, he'd learned about the old Babylonians and all the mighty kings they once had. Asiaticus was a brilliant teacher.

The slave opened a door, closed it, and left Lucius alone with Asiaticus.

The blemmye sat with his back turned to Lucius, deeply sunk into work. "Lucius," he said, not looking up, "one day I'll lose my power."

"You mean your consulship? Yes, I know, you only serve a year, and half of yours is already gone."

"Not that," Asiaticus said, continuing his writing. "*That* is something I'll have to deal with when the time is right, I will not give up just because I've been told. No, what I mean is when

I'm dead. The family must live on, must grow in strength. Do you understand?"

Lucius bit softly on his fingers. "No," he said after a moment's silence, "I'm not sure I do."

Finally, Asiaticus turned around. In his hand he held a papyrus sheet. "Lucius, I want you to be my heir. I adopt you. And stop biting on your fingers."

Lucius blinked four, five times – tried to understand why Asiaticus joked about such a thing – but the blemmye's weird body face was as grave as ever.

"What? *Me?* But you have a son. You have an heir, your own blood. He's human too! Why put me in front of him? Why make me your eldest son?"

"Partly, it's your mind," Asiaticus explained calmly. "I love my son, just as I love my wife, but no matter how I raise him, he'll never be a match for you. It takes something special to survive in this city, but most of all, it's your roots."

"My roots?"

"Yes, I know you're a Gaul, like me. I know you're the son of a chief who resisted Rome, and got killed as a result. You've had a difficult childhood, Lucius – if we should continue to call you that – not at all like my son, who was born into wealth. *He* will never understand true struggle. *He* will be devoured by the city. I had to fight just to get to Rome, fight against the mockeries of my appearance, fight to become a senator, to become a consul. Fight to become well-liked by Emperor Tiberius. Fight, just as you have done. That's why you're worthy to be my successor, worthy to be my son."

Asiaticus handed him the papyrus sheet and an ink-dipped pen. "I've prepared the contract, all you have to do is sign."

Lucius' hands trembled, but his writing lessons had paid off, and he managed to sign his name.

"Thank you, Lucius Valerius Asiaticus, my son."

XV

Apollo was victorious over the darkness yet again, and the last day of preparation had begun. Tomorrow, they would rob the Temple of Juno Moneta.

Already, half of Rome had come out to do their morning tasks. There, gray-haired city officials were on their way to the Tabularium; and there, Panotti from Scythia acted very busy, who – after bathing and hanging themselves from oak trees to dry their man-sized ears – had been caught by an unexpected storm, been taken to Rome, and only stayed when they proved to be excellent lawyers. In an attempt to avoid getting swept away by the current of shoves, Lucius pressed his back against the street-framing buildings. Despite his efforts, he wasn't quite successful, and soon found himself swimming through the crowds.

His objective for the morning lived in a hovel of peculiar architectural style. Although, actually, he could've lived perfectly decently; for Chymes – as the alchemist was called – was well funded by the debts he incurred as advances on gold orders, and by the benevolent people that borrowed him money to pay off those debts.

Already when Lucius banged on the door, which tilted upwards even though the rest of the building had sunk halfway to the underworld, he regretted not making his visit during the night. Chymes was somewhat of a nocturnal fellow that often hurled insults at those who dared wake him in the morning.

Bang, bang, bang. Finally, a hoarse voice shouted, "I'm sleeping!"

"Wake up, then," Lucius replied. "For I much desire to speak with you."

***

When Chymes opened, he ranted a while about Lucius' rudeness and lack of respect for alchemists' professionalism and need of rest. Lucius spent the time studying the kelp beard that left much of Chymes' face to the imagination. The alchemist usually claimed it was a result of a failed experiment, or, when he was in a more inventive mood, that he was half sea creature, and Lucius found the explanations good even though he knew they were false.

Somewhere between the attacks, Lucius managed to present his case. "Has he been here? The prefect? I'm sorry it was a Praetorian instead of a Vigiles, but I'm sure you can handle it."

Chymes changed his voice, as he often did when it came to business. "Perhaps, but unfortunately, my meetings are of deeply confidential nature."

"Here," Lucius said, throwing him a fairly stuffed pouch, "something I got on my way here, I'm afraid. Apart from avoiding people, I must say I don't quite get why you waste all this time on experiments. I've always found that the best way to make gold is simply by taking someone else's. Anyway, do not think you can lure more than that from me. You know very well what you will get in return once it's all over."

"You're the only pickpocket I know who doesn't like crowds," Chymes mumbled, biting every coin to ensure their authenticity. More than anyone, Chymes knew it was a lousy method, but it was a sickly habit he'd formed. "Marcus Clemens was here three days ago. A wicked thing by the by, that everyone is called Marcus in this city."

"Did he fall for it?"

"Yes, quite a lovely story you've concocted. Your calculations were very convincing."

"And the other thing?" Lucius asked.

Chymes winked somewhere behind all his kelp. "All according to instructions. Act two of the Jade Plan has begun."

***

They had gathered in Lucius' insula, after carefully ensuring that Clemens wasn't around. It was a safety risk, holding the meeting there, with the enemy next door, but Lucius deemed it necessary that Flamma knew all the details. The half-cyclops recovered better than Lucius had dared hope, but even in a seemingly crowdier Rome, he couldn't move through the city streets without his massive figure being instantly recognized.

"Welcome, all," Lucius began, "we've come a long way on our journey, but still the most important task remains – the heist. I'm sure you want to know more about this, but before we begin, Kezekem, what news from your shadowing? What's Clemens been up to?"

Kezekem lay with his back to the floor in a courageous attempt to exterminate the insula's vermin. "Not much," he said, yawning. "Oh, yeah, right, he confronted some driver."

"A driver? Appia?"

"Nah, not her. Another one. He who wins. Hostus."

"So, what did they say?"

"They spoke of the weather."

Lucius studied the sciapod. Kezekem bent his neck

to meet his gaze, as he raised his foot above his head to shield himself from the faint rays Apollo sent in through the window.

"The weather? Please don't lie. Obviously they didn't speak of the weather."

Kezekem shrugged. It looked odd, with him lying down. "Nah-uh-huh, but you told me to shadow, not listen. Shadows don't have ears. Anyhow, the driver cried, a pathetic wimp, that one."

"Well, alright," Lucius said, doubtful of the usefulness of the information. "Has Clemens done anything else?"

Kezekem shook his head. It looked even odder.

"Really? Nothing at all? What about him meeting the alchemist Chymes? Aren't you going to mention that?"

"But so what? It hasn't got anything to do with us, right? Although I was glad to be reminded of him, yeah. Nineteen quadrans he owes me. He promised he'd make 'em into gold, but d'you see any gold in my hands?"

"Chymes?" Pollio interjected. "Did he say anything about his beard?"

"Shut up!" Lucius snapped. "Kezekem, it *is* important, and I'd love to know what else Clemens has done that you don't consider important."

"Is this interrogation finished soon, amicus? I thought you were gonna present the rest of the Plan."

Lucius rolled his eyes. Sometimes – no, always – Kezekem was quite annoying. "Well, let's start by answering the following: What's the most delicate part of the heist?"

"When we sneak into the temple," Pollio guessed.

"When punch guards," Flamma suggested, his lizardwolf yapping something in agreement.

"Nope, and nope," Lucius said lightly, "it's something far more important. I speak of the escape. When we take all our coins, the whole treasure, and disappear. Think about it, without escape we're just a group of failed robbers, stopped by the mighty guardians of Rome. A group of robbers who may have placed a big bet, but lost even bigger. All of Rome will hunt us when the treasure is ours, and let me tell you a secret: seven hundred sixty-three thousand denarii are utterly bloody useless when you're thrown to the lions."

Everyone – except possibly Flamma, who was familiar with the beasts – seemed to agree, so Lucius carried on. "We'll take a chariot, big enough to carry all the sacks, and let Appia take us out of the city as quickly as possible. There are lots of roads to choose from, as you know, all lead to Rome, but the greatest of them all is our driver's namesake, Via Appia. We take that down to Sinuessa and—"

"Why horses?" Pollio said. "Why not strap Kezekem in front of the chariot, like we did when we freed Flamma? Nothing is as quick."

Lucius sighed. Always – no, sometimes – he wondered why he bothered letting Pollio be part of the work at all. "Do you have any idea how much attention we would attract? A jumping sciapod with a loaded chariot flying behind? It's true that many are in a hurry on Via Appia, but not to that degree. Besides, Kezekem wouldn't cope. First of all, he doesn't have the stamina, second, ninety bulging sacks of gold and silver will make the chariot so heavy that even Flamma would prefer not to lift it all at once."

"Hey, amicus," Kezekem protested, "'course I cope. Raced two hyenas once, though buggers. Ran all the way through Cyrenaica – won without it even being close. But speaking of Appia, where has she gone?"

"She left," Pollio said. "She—"

"Shut *up!*" Lucius snapped for the second time. He didn't want to discuss Appia. He had to find her himself. Had to sort out the problems he himself had created. Appia was crucial.

"So, Sinuessa," he said in an attempt to carry on with the Plan, "we'll start to move on minor roads there, to make it difficult for our pursuers. There's a small village by the coast where I've arranged with a punic pirate to pick us up. He'll smuggle us across Mare Nostrum, and after that, you're free to do what you desire with your fortune."

"I equip soldiers," Flamma revealed. "Colossal army. Keep cinnamon birds safe. Forever."

"Yuck, what a waste," Kezekem said. "I'll build a magnificent palace – whitest marble, bigger than anything the world has ever seen – and there I'll host a feast every day and every night, and all amici will visit me for all time and eternity. The Emperor will kiss my foot, and on top of columns scraping the sky, huge slabs of stone will keep Apollo at bay."

"Why not use it for something good?" Pollio suggested. "All those who suffer in Rome, who have no home, no food, don't they deserve a better life?"

"And Brontes will build mountain of coins," Flamma said. "There she sits and—"

"What!" Kezekem exclaimed. "Brontes? Does fungus grow in your brain or what? No way we're sharing the loot with a beast! In five we'll split it, in five!"

Don't they get it? Lucius thought as the debate raged on. *All that gold, all that silver, all that bronze, all that copper. Rome will hunt us down like cynocephali. We can never return. We can never show our faces here again.*

"What're gonna do with your share, Lucius?" Pollio asked in a poorly disguised attempt to silence the others, as Brontes too had weighed in on the matter with a mix of yaps and hisses that Flamma dutifully interpreted.

To be perfectly honest, Lucius didn't care much about his share. What he did care about was his glory, the immortal one, *immortalis gloria*. He would never be a famous statesman, never a famous commander, but he would be a famous thief.

To steal a treasure from a goddess; oh, what a name that would bring! Lucius Monetacus, that would be his name. *Lucius who defeated Moneta.* It was worth it, to be chased out of the Eternal City for such a name.

Before he could formulate his thoughts to an answer, however, he heard deep voices from down the street – voices of dwarves.

He tiptoed across the floor, the others with him, except Flamma, who dragged his feet under bent knees and hardly felt the need to become even taller. They peered out through the open window shutter.

Three dwarves of the Vigiles had just left the opposite building. They walked with determined steps toward Lucius insula, their beards swaying slightly back and forth. Further down the street, two Praetorians examined every creature they found – they asked a troll to open his mouth and pulled out his tongue – and next to them, more Vigiles watchmen. It seemed no better than the two forces working together to search the entire city.

"Kezekem," Lucius hissed between his teeth, "why didn't you tell me Clemens was doing this?"

"And how should I have known, amicus? I can't shadow him when I'm here, can I?"

"We wait!" Flamma suggested, in a voice that Lucius found very far from an appropriate volume for the situation. "Wait, then punch."

"It won't do," Lucius whispered. A missing watchmen patrol would quickly draw attention, and attention was the last thing they wanted. Unless it was controlled. "Kezekem…"

"Huh? Nah, nah, nah. I won't do it."

"Come on, it doesn't have to be anything fancy. Can't you just yell something vicious and let them chase you? Should give us enough time to get out of here."

"Too late, amicus," Kezekem said as the dwarves entered the bottom floor. Judging by the protesting sounds, they quickly searched the rooms with little regard for the residents.

"Quickly," Lucius ordered, "after me."

They slipped out of the room, feeling the stench of pig stinging their noses. "Flamma, bust the door down."

Flamma gave him a hesitant look with his big eye, but Lucius nodded. Flamma put his shoulders against the door and gave it a push. It flew in, splinters swirling in the air.

Flamma clapped his hands. "I did it! I strong!"

Lucius smirked. Even Pollio could've busted down that door. And for Flamma... well, it would've been harder for an elephant to crush an amphora with its feet.

They went in. Clemens' room was nearly identical to Lucius'; a small window and little else, the only difference being that Clemens' mattress was intact. But right now, Lucius didn't care much about the decor.

"What's the point of this?" Pollio said. "We aren't any safer here than at your place."

"Give me a hand," Lucius said, grabbing the door. They tried lifting it back to its original position, but it immediately fell back down. "We'll have to keep it in place ourselves," Lucius noted.

They made the door stand upright, balanced it with their hands, and heard steps and clatter of swords outside.

"Let's start there," a voice said. "It's open."

"What, no one here?" another one said. "Could've sworn I heard a crack. And who leaves their door wide open when they leave."

"You know the filth who lives here," a third said, and then yelled, "The Gods! A lizardwolf! What's that thing doing here!"

Brontes hissed. Stumbling steps sounded as the intruders backed out of the room and ran down the stairs. *Imagine being that scared of a lizardwolf*, Lucius thought with amusement.

"Very well then," he said, "let's resume our meeting. We have a few more things to discuss."

***

"You probably wonder how we'll get into the temple," Lucius said when they returned to his room. To get their attention, he swept his gaze over his companions. Against his will, he got stuck on Flamma, who, very pleased with himself, scratched Brontes behind something that supposedly was meant to be ears. "With a hundred Praetorians and more at that, it might seem impossible; but people get in every day. We just have to do it like them. Like the priests."

"Can't," Flamma said, not looking up from his beast. "We no priests."

"Correct, but we can pretend. Personally, I'm no master of disguise, but a good friend has taught me a thing or two about the art form. Rome has far too many temples for the priests to keep track of themselves."

"Can't," Flamma repeated. "Me not dressing up. Same reason Kez won't wear boots. Shoemakers won't make. Too expensive."

"What!" Kezekem exclaimed with such force that he almost flew up from the floor where he lay. "That's not why at all, I swear! I *want* to be barefoot! How else could I wiggle my toes!" And he moved them up, down, and sideways like he was playing an invisible cithara.

"Yes, why," Flamma insisted. "I know. Clothes hard to get. Never fit. Always small. Not dressing up."

Lucius nodded. "We'll figure something out. You're too

easily recognized anyway. The real problem is the Praetorians. We'll have to distract them."

"They're relentless," Pollio said somberly. "Your distraction won't even budge their horns. Not a chance they let five unknown priests, one with a missing eye and one with a missing leg, run straight past them and into the very place they have been so strictly ordered to guard."

Lucius smiled. "Don't worry about that. In the end, the Praetorians have one task more important than all the rest, one task that is the reason for their existence, and which would cause chaos within their ranks were it disrupted. To protect the Emperor. And in this, they will fail. It's time to raise the stakes."

XVI

Clemens had asked hundreds of people before finding Thrakatulus – the dwarf whose face still was of shades deviating from the natural range – and it had taken a great deal of persuasion before the dwarf had agreed to help Clemens. Then he'd mobilized all available Praetorians, and instructed both them, and the watchmen Thrakatulus had provided, how to proceed with the investigation. The forces had learned the descriptions of the Gladiator Thieves, and so they'd set off with mixed enthusiasm. Perhaps an exaggerated measure for catching a few thieves, but Clemens thought it best to do what was necessary to avoid incurring the wrath of the Emperor.

Despite turning the entire city upside down, the catch so far had been poor. One abnormally large cooper, who'd lost an eye in a brawl in his youth; one shadowfoot with a wart the shape of an aqueduct on his foot, and a watertight alibi for the night in question.

Thus, Clemens looked forward to returning to his insula, throwing himself on his mattress and taking a breather. Perhaps with rest, his thoughts would clear and the next step in the process reveal itself. He stopped at a stand on the way, buying a piece of bread made of emmer wheat and soaked in melted cheese. He chewed and chewed, and once the bread had gone down and up his stomachs, he chewed it anew. To help his thoughts, he washed it down with some wine.

Already when he put his hoof on the first step, he felt that something was wrong, and when he got up from the stairs he realized why. His door had cracked and lay discarded on the floor. A collection of muddy footprints revealed that someone had used the opportunity to pay a visit.

He lowered his head, pointing his horns forward, cursed his stomping steps, and entered the room. No one there, the burglar was gone. If it had *been* a burglar, for everything seemed to be in order. Odd, a smashed door and nothing else.

Saturn! My mattress!

The burglar had torn it apart. Or no, not torn, *squashed* it until the seams burst and reeds stuck up in all directions.

Clemens sighed, sat down on the mattress, pulled the straws, and contemplated the situation. His new neighbor, hadn't he seemed a bit shady? Something about his face felt off. But why would he…

Then it hit him.

Vigiles! Those dimwits searched my room! A depressing thought, but he couldn't really blame them for doing as told. Although he did find it incomprehensible how they could believe the Gladiator Thieves were hiding in the mattress.

"*Ave, praefectus.*"

Clemens turned around. He'd been so absorbed in thought, that he hadn't noticed the visitor. One of his Praetorians.

"Yes?"

"The Emperor wishes to see you."

***

As Clemens strode through the palace halls, he thought about his report. The Emperor would demand results from the investigation – his mind was at times difficult to guess, but that much Clemens understood.

The Emperor lay and ate. Slaves stuffed him with grapes, wine, and geese. "Explain yourself," he said through gobbling bites.

Clemens tried. He admitted to not having caught anyone yet, but was following a lead, confident in finding the thieves soon.

"Give it to me," the Emperor interrupted.

"It?" Clemens said. "Your Godliness means the Gladiator Thieves?"

"The stone," the Emperor growled. "The Jadecrystal. It has called to me, Jupiter, King of Gods. I need it for my scepter, or it cannot keep the thunder in check. You have hid it from me – hand it over immediately, and I shall consider not executing you."

Clemens felt as if he'd sunk into a swamp of icy water. *How does he know? How? I hardly know myself. I… Chymes! That bastard sold me out!* The crystal quivered in his pocket. Screaming to stay, to not be handed to the Emperor. Giving such a maniac even more power could never end well.

His hands burned as he picked it up. The Jadecrystal crackled and sparked. So small, and so powerful.

The Emperor snatched it from him.

XVII

Appia hadn't eaten, hadn't slept. Just strolled about, breathing freedom. She told herself it was because she was above such trivial needs, that her freedom was all she needed and desired, but now her stomach rumbled. Last night, when the cold came with sharpened claws, she'd found an empty spot under an aqueduct but barely closed her eyes before being chased off by the Vigiles.

All she knew was how to ride, but she couldn't return to the stable. Never again would she let herself be shackled by its chains.

On the street she heard of curious things. A divine stone had appeared in Rome. The Praetorians had seized it, hidden it from the Emperor and conspired against him. Appia almost felt sorry for them – it wasn't hard to figure out how the Emperor would react.

And they spoke about tomorrow, about who would be appointed consul. Appia was annoyed by the mere thought.

At least the thirst wasn't an issue. At every intersection, fountains gushed fresh water from the many aqueducts that led to the city. But her stomach tore her insides. She had to eat *something*.

She pushed her way into the crowd at the Forum. The

merchants sold their last goods of the day, and still there were plenty of customers. Unusually plenty of customers, Appia reckoned, but that was probably because she normally trained at the stable at this hour.

"Fresh delicacies! Straight from the Tiber!"

Appia managed to squirm close enough to catch a glimpse of the merchant's iron bucket. In it, a weary crabb and a dozen of three-headed tadpoles splashed around. At a stand further away, another merchant sold bread, and while he was busy with a customer, Appia pulled out her falx knife and cut half a loaf for herself.

Someone put a hand on her shoulder.

The Praetorians! she thought, growing cold. The punishment for theft wasn't severe, just a fine four times the value stolen – the Laws of the Twelve Tables were falling out of fashion, and drowning and beheading was no longer considered appropriate for such a minor offense – but when Appia couldn't afford even that, what would happen? She knew. They would enslave her again.

She turned around, clutching her knife. There – up close, the only way to talk at the Forum – stood a short man, holding his sore fingers over his forehead in protection from the afternoon sun. Or rather, in protection from prying eyes.

"Well, well, well, look who's become a thief," Lucius said.

Appia shook his hand off her shoulder. "What do you want?" she snapped, angrier than she intended to.

"You know that already."

"Is that so? Then *you* already know the answer. I won't help those who I cannot trust."

"Here," Lucius said, briefly exposing his face by handing over a sack as large as himself. "Something to quell the hunger with."

Appia peeked in the sack. Carrots, bread, olives, grain, cheese, grapes, and something long and blue – a boiled horn of eale, the sturdy, beastly oxen that grazed the far away fields of Salento.

"Did you really believe you could buy me with this?" The confidence in her voice surprised even her; she'd never smelled anything as good.

"Well," Lucius said with a smile, sweeping down a lock of hair over his forehead, "I didn't pay for it either."

Appia threw her stolen half loaf into the sack, and followed Lucius away from the square. They weren't alone – that wasn't an easily achieved state in the city – but were at least spared from the worst crowds.

"I won't do it," Appia said, once they could speak more privately. "I'm free."

"You're not free from your word. You had your chance to say no, during our first meeting in the catacombs, but you said *yes*. Do not break your promise now."

"That was when you promised I'd win, wasn't it? We both know what happened to that promise."

Lucius frowned deeply, wrinkles coating his face in a way that suddenly made him seem several years older. "It was stupid. I… sorry. But you have to, Appia. You *have to*. We can't do without you. You are chosen."

"Yes, I know."

Lucius started. "You *know*?"

"Yes, you chose me because I'm the best driver in Rome." When she said it aloud, the stupidity of it struck her. "No," she whispered, hurt by the realization, "not the best. The *cheapest*."

Lucius' eyes narrowed. Green with streaks of yellow, like freshly fallen leaves. How could they be so false? How could they break every promise without a blink? "You're not chosen by me, but by Jupiter. You are the one foretold by the Vestal. It has to be you."

"Jupiter? Nice try, but it doesn't matter what you say. I'm not with you anymore."

"Fine," Lucius hissed. "I won't convince you. Not here. Not when they hunt us." And he disappeared into the crowds.

***

Lucius stormed through Rome, for once not caring about the pushes he got. Appia had abandoned them. Lucius still didn't understand. How could Jupiter's chosen abandon them? And on the eve of the great day, at that?

Well, there was no time to convince Appia. The heist must happen tomorrow. Not just because the Praetorians were on to them, the day suited the Plan all too well to pass up. The Emperor would host a feast at the Circus; his throat would be exposed.

But they needed a driver. There was only one who could compare to Appia, one who always won the races – one named Hostus.

It's a risk, Lucius thought, slowing his pace. Hostus had talked to Clemens, to the enemy, and according to Kezekem, Hostus was a pathetic wimp. What kept him from revealing the whole scheme? From crying to the Praetorians and having them all executed? Would they really put their trust in a stranger?

Yes, Appia had made sure there was no other option. Damned chosen ones and their ideas.

Besides, there was one detail that made it far too tempting, too irresistible, to not choose Hostus – his horse was the reason for the feast. The Emperor would gather all of Rome at the Circus, in a great ceremony to celebrate himself as Jupiter. And there, he would elevate Incitatus to the highest office besides himself.

He would make Incitatus a consul.

Lucius hoped everyone would be ready by then, friend and foe alike. For they wouldn't just steal the Treasure of Juno Moneta; they would steal the Emperor's favorite horse before his dying eyes.

XVIII

Clemens felt helpless and vacant. He took a few gulps of wine, letting the thick sludge run down his throat as he lay on his squashed mattress, staring at the thornlarvas trying to escape the cobwebs on the ceiling. They wriggled and shot out their thorns, but every movement only entangled them more. More gulps. Clemens preferred wine to food, since it remained in his stomachs on the first try, but now, all taste was gone.

He hadn't thought much about the Jadecrystal when it was in his possession, doubting its powers, not caring. But now, that it was gone, forever out of reach, the Jadecrystal called to him. His chest burned, his head pounded, his vision oscillated between being blurred and sharpened. Was this how the Babylonian king, Esarhaddon, had felt? Was this the feeling that made him crush the mighty Egyptian Empire?

Clemens had held the crystal in his hands. Several days he'd carried it with him, owned it – and then, he'd given it away. Why! He could've refused, he could've fought his way free, he could've…

No, there was nothing he could have done. And if there ever was, it didn't matter. You couldn't reverse time like an hourglass.

I might have been able to, with the Jadecrystal. What had

Chymes said that the crystal could do? It contained ancient Egyptian powers, but what did that mean?

Chymes! Clemens didn't know why he'd trusted that rascal in the first place. If it was one thing that all of Rome agreed on, it was how devious the kelp-haired alchemist was, how he wriggled and squirmed, tricking everyone he came across. Clemens should've known better.

In every ear in Rome, they whispered of the prefect who'd stolen from the Emperor. It could only mean death. How could Clemens ever have thought otherwise? How could he have thought that the Emperor would forgive someone who'd hidden such a treasure?

Jupiter was merciless.

He didn't think he'd be strangled, like most people, nor be stomped to death by his Praetorians. No, Clemens was convinced – *knew* – that he would be flung down Tarpeian Rock. Feel his head smash against the ground, spine stick out of his back and guts slither out of his body like eels.

Tarpeian Rock – the cliff at the top of Capitoline Hill where Rome's most vile criminals were punished. Traitors, notorious murderers, slave rebellion leaders… all soared through the air before they hit the ground, their blood flooding the streets like the shame that would never be washed from their name.

Clemens choked on the wine. Coughed and beat his chest. His chest that burned with the call of the Jadercystal.

He had intended to throw the Gladiator Thieves off the cliff, the ones who'd caused all this misery; instead, he would be the one to end his days there. He shivered and felt sick. Oh, how he felt sick.

I'm never sick, he thought. *More wine, Bacchus!*

Tomorrow, the Emperor would host a feast at the Circus. And there, he would make a horse – actually a unicorn – consul. The Senate would get a new leader, and Clemens wondered what the senators would think of their new boss.

It doesn't matter what they think. The Emperor had the power, the Emperor did as the Emperor desired. For Clemens, there was nothing to do but wait.

It knocked on the door.

That was quick, Clemens thought, rising from the mattress on shaky hooves. He looked at the door. Right, it lay on the ground in memory of the ravages of the Vigiles. Whoever had come for him must've knocked on the wall.

Anyhow, a man stood there, but – Clemens noted in surprise – not a soldier. Instead, it was a very peculiar fellow, with long eyebrows, short black hair, and a thin but distinct mustache hanging over his upper lip. He was dressed in a voluminous rose-colored robe with black ribbons. Not a common tunic, not even a toga; Clemens had never seen anything like it.

"Good evening," the stranger said in broken Latin. Clemens tried to determine from which province the dialect originated, but the wine appeared to prevent him from such analyses. "My name is Ma Kuang," the stranger continued, letting his dress flow together by sliding each hand to the other sleeve.

"So?" Clemens said, trying to make his voice sound as firm as usual.

Ma Kuang coughed. "Always so direct, you *yaoguai*. I don't blame you, even the humans here seem to have such traits. I represent a group – a community of honorable individuals – I offer them my humble help. They have a mission of a most delicate nature."

Get to the point, Clemens thought, not bothering to say anything. The fever had increased with the visit of the stranger. Waves crashed against his body with a steady rhythm. A message from the Jadecrystal.

"Unfortunately, the group has been suffering from

quite demeaning treatment lately; treatment that is hurting the *dignitas* of which they are so very fond. Perhaps you could be of assistance in our efforts to prevent more of such things."

Clemens understood, and was annoyed to be bothered with such a petty matter. "Look, if the Vigiles have been careless in searching the city, you'll have to take it up with them. I don't really care whose villa they smashed. Go complain to *their* prefect instead, a certain Thrakatulus. The Praetorians have carried out their duty with the respect of which they're known."

"Oh, it's not dwarves that're bothering my friends. It's the Emperor."

"The Emperor? But—"

"We demand nothing major of you," Ma Kuang said with a smile, "merely that you momentarily refrain from your ordinary duties."

Nothing major, Clemens thought, staring at the stranger, *only the worst atrocity a prefect can commit.* If it was one thing that most certainly would get him flung down Tarpeian Rock, it was this.

The world spun. Everything moved except Ma Kuang's smile in the center of it all. Clemens thought of the Emperor's madness, of how he would abuse the power of the Jadecrystal, of what Clemens himself could have accomplished if he'd kept what rightfully belonged to him. He could have made all of Rome a better place. He could have made the Capture undone.

"No," he said, surprised by his words, "I will not stand and watch as you murder my Emperor. Let me share the knife."

***

Clemens stayed up all night, working in companion with his wine. Every detail had to be thought through, how it would happen, which Praetorians Clemens would place closest to the

Emperor, where he would commit the stabbing. The decision had given him a strange sense of clarity.

He selected a few suitable Praetorians in his mind, and decided to talk to them before the feast tomorrow. The rest of the Guard, Clemens decided, would be at the Circus too; they had to witness Rome's transformation with their own eyes to understand.

Ma Kuang had listed some of those involved in the plot, to make Clemens know who his friends were. Among them were powerful senators like the relatives Marcus Vinicius and Annius Vinicianus, countless of the Emperor's closest men, and several high-ranking military officers whom Clemens assumed had joined due to the legate who was stomped to death last week by the Emperor's orders.

And I can stop them all. Unbelievable, really. Ma Kuang had given him hard and fast evidence. All Clemens had to do was whisper in the Emperor's ear, and everything would be stopped in its tracks with the conspirators flung down Tarpeian Rock. Clemens would be cleared of all suspicion, forever having a place by the Emperor's side.

From which I'd see the Jadecrystal, Clemens thought. *Day in and day out it would be so close and so out of reach.*

Later that night, he had another visit. But this time it was Hostus, the driver who'd promised to help Clemens find the Gladiator Thieves.

Hostus' face was covered in sweat, eyes watery, breath choppy and heavy. He immediately began yapping about being contacted by a short stranger with black, curly hair, who introduced himself as Turpilinus. Apparently, Hostus had been hired as a driver for Turplinus and his friends; they sought a quick way out of the city.

Clemens waved the driver off. He was too busy with his planes to be disturbed.

Hostus threw out his arms. "But h-he had a wart on his forehead! I h-heard the Vigiles talk about it when they searched the city. A wart on his forehead, it was h-he who stole the gladiator! I'm sure of it!"

Clemens felt as if he'd sunk into a swamp of horse dung. "Tell me again what you were going to do?"

"Prepare a h-horse and large chariot. Then pick them up in a place they'd reveal later. H-he wouldn't give any details, but I think they plan to strike again. Another theft."

Clemens' posterior heart beat faster, his front one harder; as if his body tried to rip him to pieces. *Another theft.* What would they steal now? The Gladiator Theft had seemed so carefully plotted, so brave. Even though he hated his opponents, Clemens couldn't help but admire their craftsmanship. And he felt a strong urge to stop them. For he was better than them.

"When?"

"Tomorrow," Hostus said. "In the evening."

By Saturn, why tomorrow? Any other day and Clemens could've stopped it, but not tomorrow. Why did it annoy him so badly? Catching the Gladiator Thieves was a task he'd gotten from the Emperor, the same Emperor he was about to assassinate. What did it matter?

You know it matters. He couldn't give up what he had fought for, it wasn't *right*. But he had to. Stopping the Emperor was so much bigger than catching a gang of thieves, so much bigger than anything.

He got an idea.

"Do as this Turpilinus asked you. Wait where they tell you, with chariot and horses. Your unicorn too, don't bother going to the Circus. Yes, I *forbid* you from going there. Wait for the thieves, let them on your chariot, and ride off."

Hostus looked as if he would object, but Clemens forestalled him. "Don't go where they tell you to go. Instead, head to the Circus. There, I'll wait with my guard and the lions. The crowd might need some entertainment to digest what will have happened there."

"But the Emperor!" Hostus cried. "What will the Emperor say! A feast for Incitatus, and I'm not there with him. He'll h-hate me."

Clemens took a step closer. The driver backed away, his eyes as frightened as when they first met. "Then may he hate you. Just remember, it's not the Emperor, but me you shall fear. Do as I've told you, Hostus. Or the world will know your horse is a unicorn."

Hostus stuttered something affirmative and practically ran away.

The Gods, Clemens thought, taking a gulp of wine, *what a day that awaits Rome tomorrow.*

XIX

Six years earlier

Yet again, Lucius had to throng with those he despised, with those who were at the Circus just like him – in Apollo's ruthless summer heat, at that. Curtains had been stretched as a roof to shade the arena, but the heat didn't care, the air stifling in a way only the air of Rome could be. The race preparations were well underway, and in the meantime, the leprechaun was calling out numbers in a cone. Lucius squeezed his new, green stone, the one that would give him luck. He had named it the Jadecrystal.

Life wasn't that bad, anyway. Last time his creditors had attacked him, they'd found out that Lucius wasn't called Turpilinus anymore, but Valerius Asiaticus, and been kind enough to give him a two-week reprieve; while sevenfolding his debt to a total of two hundred fifty denarii. It was quite a fortune, but the extra time had proved useful and eventually Lucius had found a way to pay off the debt. A weight had been lifted from his shoulders.

The new one is far heavier, he thought, but told himself he would find a solution. He always did.

"Thirteen, forty-nine, seven…"

Lucius crumpled his lottery ticket and threw it away.

The Jadecrystal hadn't helped, of course it hadn't. How could it help something that was impossible to help? To play on Green Gnaeus' lottery was to lose.

Lucius glared down at the disgusting leprechaun, who just burst into laughter as if satisfied to have swindled a hundred thousand Romans out of whatever spare change they had. Or didn't have.

That's the last quadrans you got from me, he thought, making his way through the sweaty spectators who yelled for the race to begin. *Never ever that you'll fool me again.*

Yesterday, he'd promised the same thing. But this time it was different.

***

The knot in his stomach grew with every step toward home. Walking up Pincian Hill had never felt as heavy, and that wasn't solely due to the heat. When he finally reached the top, he thought he saw faces in the plants of the garden: wet mourning eyes, and sharp grinning teeth.

Asiaticus stood alone by the cherry tree. Or, by what remained of it.

"What happened!" Lucius said, jogging to his father. "The tree! It's ruined!"

The cherry tree had shriveled and rotted all the way down to its roots. Not a leaf was to be seen, and twigs had grayed and fallen to the ground.

"Someone picked its fruit, before the time was right," Asiaticus said, standing with his back slumped. "The tree died of sorrow, losing its children like that."

Lucius' heart stopped, preparing for an extra hard beat; it pulsed two fast beats and stopped again. He licked his lips. "But that's horrible."

Asiaticus didn't answer.

"Why? Who could've done this to you? A gardener? A political rival, seeking your consulship?"

When Asiaticus spoke, it was no longer a summer day. A mist, cold as the abyss, had hidden in his stomach, and was now leaking from his mouth for the first time.

"You can stop pretending. I know who it was. It's not easy, selling the world's most exotic fruit on the street without people's chatter."

Lucius felt tears burning their way up his face. "I'm sorry. Please, I didn't know. I swear by Jupiter, by Juno, by Minerva – I didn't know! I didn't know the tree would die, I needed the fruit. I needed it."

"I can tolerate a lot, Lucius. But never people who betray my trust. It's too valuable to be wasted. Get out of my sight. For good."

"But—"

"Leave. You were never my son."

XX

The day had come. The day that everything had led up to, from that rainy afternoon lottery, when Lucius got his idea, to the sleepless nights of planning, and finally the gathering of the crew. Now, all was in place. All but Appia.

"Too hard," Flamma complained from his stretcher. "Barely breathe."

"Well, it's easier to play dead if you actually are," Lucius said, further tightening the bandages. "Besides, you are a half-cyclops – some cloth can hardly hurt you."

Before Flamma raised any further objections, Kezekem returned. The sciapod wore a leather dress similar to those typically worn by the sacred butchers. It was decorated with finger-long, crooked fangs that rattled as he jumped.

"All set at the Emperor's feast, amicus. The Circus is brimming with spectators, and everywhere Praetorians are trying to bring order. And best of all – Green Gnaeus is holding a lottery. The whole crowd's playing."

"Good for them," Lucius said, hearing the Circus rumbling in the distance. No, he wouldn't rush over with a lottery ticket. He wouldn't!

It was that time again. Lucius in front, Pollio and Kezekem in the back. Arms, legs, spine – his whole body – ached under the weight. Lucius was sure his bones would crumble, leaving nothing but dust. He wasn't built for lifting Flamma, not even with a stretcher. Although, naturally, no one was.

And in no way was it made easier by Lucius' attire. A stringy, white priest-toga that constantly reminded itself by entangling both arms and legs. If this was a master disguise, Lucius wanted nothing more to do with the art form.

The Temple of Juno Moneta rose above the surroundings as they crept closer. Beautiful and terrifying. To rest, they put Flamma down, and Pollio seized the opportunity to vomit out some dreadful tones from his flute; he claimed to have practiced the instrument the entire previous day, to really grow comfortable in his role as a flutist, but all his efforts had come to naught.

"Not even the deaf are gonna believe that," Kezekem said.

Pollio seemed hurt, but unfortunately, Lucius found no reason to doubt the sciapod's analysis. "Play only if absolutely necessary," he ordered.

Despite the allure of the Circus, disturbingly many people lingered in the small square outside the temple. Every day – every hour, even – the city swelled like an overfermented dough, and nowhere were you safe from the jostling masses.

No ceremony had been held, however, and by the gate, one Praetorian did guard duty rather than four.

"Halt!" the Praetorian said as they approached with Flamma once more hovering between them in a most toilsome manner. "I know you, who are you?"

The one who stuck his tongue out, Lucius thought smugly, but said, "Of course you know me, I'm a priest of this temple."

"You are, eh? But all priests should work at the Circus today. You're needed for the feast."

"We carry a dead," Lucius exhaled under the weight of said burden, "to tend to in the temple."

"Eh? Sounds like an unusual task for a priest." The Praetorian spotted Brontes slithering under the stretcher. "A lizardwolf? Repulsive beast! That thing won't get in here alive."

There was a deep rumble from Flamma, but the Praetorian didn't seem to notice.

"The creature will fall from my axe," Kezekem said. "We sacrifice inside today, too many people out on the square."

Only now did the Praetorian notice Kezekem. "A shadowfoot? As *victimarius*? You shouldn't be on sacred ground!" He paused and added, "I don't suppose you know anything about the shadowfoot involved in the Gladiator Theft the other night? There's been a massive search for him."

Kezekem raised his voice. "You think I'm friends with every sciapod in Rome? Don't you know how big this city is! What would you say if I assumed that the rogue faun who left the Praetorian Guard and is leading rebellions in Noricum is your brother?"

A faint reddish tone appeared on the Praetorians sideburned cheeks. He briefly glanced down, and opened the gate. This time, Lucius didn't stick out his tongue.

"You know so much," Pollio whispered to Kezekem. "I've never even heard of a rogue faun leading rebellions in Noricum."

Kezekem grinned. "Me neither."

When the gate slammed shut behind them, all went quiet. The temple was fully deserted, not a priest, not a coinsmith, not a Praetorian. The feast of the Circus was far too enticing.

Finally, they put Flammas stretcher down. Lucius arms were broken sticks, his chest burning, legs lifeless lumps; but they'd made it. They were inside the temple, the hard part was over.

Fearing Flamma would tire of being dead, breaking free from his cloth shackles on his own, they hurriedly untangled

Flamma's bandages and carefully folded them. Kezekem had come up with the idea, the bandages doubling as sacks to carry the loot. The sciapod had always seemed keen on the financial aspects of the heist.

Despite Lucius wanting nothing more than to tear off his toga, he forced himself to keep his disguise just a little longer. He led the way deeper into the temple, to the statue with marble of moonlight, of sunlight, of wonderful color. To Juno Moneta. *It's almost wrong to rob her*, Lucius thought, but instantly corrected himself. *It's not Moneta we're robbing. It's Green Gnaeus.* But still, it *was* the goddess' temple.

Pollio and Flamma stopped before the statue with reverent faces – even Brontes paused her eager yaps of welcoming her master back to the world of the living – but Kezekem passed right by, poking the bags of uncoined metal stacked up against the wall behind.

"Stop that will you," Lucius said. "Remember why we're here. For Green Gnaeus' lottery money, for the Treasure of Juno Moneta. Not for some scraps of metal."

Kezekem looked as if he wanted to discuss the matter, but gave up when Lucius turned his attention to the dark trapdoor in the corner of the temple that held such an enigmatic invitation to the underground.

Lucius knocked on the trapdoor as planned. Five hard knocks, like he had seen the *victimarius* do, but no one opened. He did it again – still no reaction. He tried to push his nails in the gap between the door and the floor, but discovered he'd bitten off too much of them. He was just about to ask Flamma for help when a whisper was heard.

"The little soldier boot rules Rome, but in what socks?"

Socks? Dis, how did I miss this! Lucius signaled the others to keep quiet.

"Sorry," he said, "but I've forgotten the code."

It took a while before the voice on the other side answered, and when it did, it dragged every syllable in classic doubtful manner. "Is that you, Gaius Bonus? Have you already forgotten the new password?"

Lucius nearly stumbled out a yes, but then he reconsidered. *What kind of top-security temple settles for a simple yes? It must be a trap.*

What was it Chymes had said? Everyone is called Marcus in this city.

"No," Lucius said, "it's Marcus. I was at the Circus."

"That's just like you..." the voice murmured as the trapdoor squeaked from being unlocked from the inside. It shook, fell in, and revealed a ladder down to a stoned room with torches burning on the walls. And a priest squinting up with a surprised look on his face.

Smack! Lucius landed directly on the priest. Before the priest could get up, Lucius gave him a punch with his fists that made his knuckles crack.

"Sorry, pal," he said when he, despite the nosebleed, recognized the knocked out face as the priest who'd shown him Moneta's statue.

"Why did you force us to lug the half-cyclops around?" Kezekem said, already standing next to Lucius, handing him a piece of rope. "You seem to fight just fine on your own, amicus."

Lucius snorted, tying up the priest. He almost felt sorry for him; all he'd done was open the temple for Lucius – twice even – and as a reward, he got a crooked nose and bound hands and feet.

Pollio took the ladder down. Flamma jumped and landed with a thud that shook the ground, and, judging by his agile movements, he was completely healed from his wounds. Incredible what half an hour wrapped up in bandages could do. He held the sacks bundled up under his arm, and in his right hand, he wielded the most terrible sledgehammer in Rome. (Lucius had made thorough enquiries on the matter; after all, he'd bought it for his own honestly stolen denarii.) Last of all came Brontes, with her tongue hanging out of her mouth, and her mangy tail in a slithering wag.

Built into the wall, next to the ladder, was an installation of lever and chains. Lucius pulled the lever, and the trapdoor closed above them in a satisfying manner. All light came from the flickering red glow of the torches, which – much to the dismay of Lucius' nose – were dipped in sulfur and tallow to prolong their burning.

Lucius took a torch, sweeping it in front of him to inspect the room: round, like the bottom of a well, with black, shiny stones. And a passage leading off.

"Well," he said, "that way, I suppose."

Kezekem halted, the teeths on his dress quieting. "Huh, amicus? *Suppose?* You do have a plan, don't you?"

"Of course," Lucius replied. "What kind of leader drags his friends into the underground if he doesn't have a *plan*? The treasure's in here. It can't be far."

Pollio gave him a meaningful look. He understood. There was nothing but darkness now.

XXI

Clemens couldn't tell if the Jadecrystal had stopped calling to him – now, that he'd answered its cry for help – or, if he'd simply gotten used to the pulse, but either way, he felt much better than yesterday. All he felt was a slight nausea. The wine's fault, perhaps.

It was a peaceful afternoon the Emperor had chosen for the feast. The wind defined as a gentle breeze, the air slightly warmer than it had been the last couple of days. And the Circus roared. Beasts, gladiators, crowds – all emptying their lungs.

All the senators were there, sitting on the bottom rows, not far from Clemens, with their togas gleaming white. Clemens studied their faces. They had stretched mouths, bent eyebrows, and creases in their foreheads. Did they know what was coming? Were they all privy to the conspiracy – despite Ma Kuang only mentioning some of their names – or were they simply concerned about the Emperor's intention to appoint a horse as their superior?

Despite their grim faces, many of them enjoyed the fight between the wounded lion and the cynocephalus that took place in the middle of the Circus.

"Aim for the throat! The throat!" a senator shouted with a high pitched voice, as the cynocephalus growled with its dogface, approaching the lion with the sword from a dead gladiator. Cynocephali weren't particularly intelligent, but they could imitate human movements they'd recently observed, and the gladiator *had* swung his sword quite well before a seven-legged bird shoved its beak into his neck and slurped up his spine.

Behind Rome's elite was row after row of plebs in dirty, worn rags. They cheered just as loudly as the senators when the cynocephalus dodged the lion's leap and managed to disembowel the beast with its new weapon.

The victory was short-lived. More beasts were let loose, and the fight resumed. Clemens looked away with disgust. Wasn't it time for Emperor to end the games? But no, Incitatus' ascension to consul wasn't due until the last hour before sunset.

A few steps up, in his personal box, on his special portable ivory chair – his *sella curulis* – which admittedly was highly symbolic but whose main characteristic seemed to be its uncomfortability, sat the Emperor; surrounded by Praetorians who guarded him and slaves who fed him. And next to the Emperor sat ex-consul Valerius Asiaticus, who'd been specifically invited. Clemens shook his head. He found it remarkable that Asiaticus had accepted, given how the Emperor had treated him. Or rather, given how the Emperor had treated his wife. Of all executions Clemens had carried out, that one felt the least just.

Saturn, had *any* execution been just?

Yet, there Valerius Asiaticus sat, flanking the Emperor, his blemmyish face betraying no emotion. Whether it was proof that the Emperor had everyone in his grip, or that Asiaticus would stop at nothing to maintain his political power, Clemens couldn't tell.

I wonder how he'll react when the Emperor gets attacked.

The Emperor looked truly majestic for the day. His thin, light brown hair swept down just over his forehead, and his tasteless beginnings of a beard – an attempt to mimic Jupiter – did little to spoil the image, as all eyes were drawn to what he held in his hand. There, from his right hand down to the ground, was a twisted staff of exceptional quality. The work of a true master, a scepter of elegant silver, and at the top – a few feet above the Emperor's head – wreathed in carved symbols of gold, sparkling like a green sun, like a star, like the light of Apollo or Jupiter's lightnings, was the Jadecrystal.

Clemens' breath grew heavy as his eyes settled on what he'd given away, on what was *his*. The crystal called to him again, pulsing with a deep, dark green glow. He could take it, right at this moment. Order the Praetorians to step aside, thrust a sword through the Emperor's stomach, and tear out the Jadecrystal from the scepter that was a mockery to its power. So close...

He forced his gaze away. Best not to be tempted, not to attract attention. The time had not yet come, the assassination must wait until the appointment. Ma Kuang had been very clear on the matter, even if he'd refused to explain why.

Clemens wondered how his fellow conspirators would react when they discovered that he planned to take the Jadecrystal for himself. It would probably result in a fight, although Clemens' experience told him humans seldom engaged in voluntary combat with a faun.

Trying to avoid both the temptation of the Jadecrystal, and the sickening slaughter in the middle of the Circus, Clemens once more turned his attention to the men sitting on the lower rows of the Circus. There, Annius Vinicianus conversed with his uncle Marcus Vinicius, both of them with mouths that barely opened. Annius immediately turned his head, staring Clemens straight in the eye.

Clemens shuddered. More and more he felt he'd chosen the right team; it was a dangerous group he was dealing with, not the kind you'd want as enemies. Especially Ma Kuang, who was nowhere to be seen. That didn't surprise Clemens. Based on what little he knew about the stranger, he didn't seem like the type who stood in the foreground.

Yes, they are dangerous, he thought, *but I was wrong. They will not fight for the Jadecrystal. It's just a jewel to them. Incredibly valuable and magnificent, but just a jewel. They don't know what it truly is. They don't know what it can do.*

Of course, Clemens didn't know that either. Only that it had crushed the Egyptian Empire.

In a way, it's going to crush ours too.

It couldn't be long now. An hour, judging by the sundial outside the Emperor's box. Then, slaves would go fetch Incitatus and Hostus, only to discover that both unicorn and driver were missing. That they stood waiting for a crew of criminals.

Yet another thing Clemens' fellow conspirators would be upset about. So be it – Clemens wouldn't let the damn thieves get away.

XXII

The beast bellowed and threw up its head, fourteen horns sprouting from the holes in its skull.

"What *is* that thing?" Pollio said with a revulsion Lucius gladly shared.

"What do I know?" Lucius said, despite there being something familiar about the beast. *Dis*, he thought, *I've seen an image of you, haven't I? Many years ago. Why didn't it explain how to beat you?*

Flamma roared, throwing himself into battle with his sledgehammer in both hands. He aimed for the belly – a big gray ball of slush in the middle of it – but the beast gasped violently, moving its belly further up and making Flamma narrowly miss.

The beast unfolded its black, bat-like wings and flapped so fiercely that Flamma was blown back by the wind. Flamma quickly got to his feet, but even then he looked small compared to his opponent.

"Shouldn't we help him?" Pollio said, where they stood a few steps away.

"Nah," Kezekem said, "we wouldn't wanna disturb our fighter when he's at his busiest. Right, amicus?"

"Right," Lucius replied, "seems stupid."

"Would not disturb!" Flamma shouted as he dodged a

bite attack from the beast.

"Did you hear something, Kezekem?"

"Huh? Nah, nothing."

Flamma landed a blow to the beast's waist. Shells shattered, and one of its spider legs came off and fell to the ground. The beast limped. Apparently it had three or four additional legs, but it howled in pain.

Flamma jumped to the side, breaking off another leg. The beast fell to the ground. Knocked out.

"Victory!" Flamma said, facing his companions. There was a red sparkle in his black eye.

Lucius, pretending he was at the Circus, threw out his right arm with force, pointing his thumb directly at the fighters. Flamma raised his hammer in salute, and turned to the beast, ready to crush its meaningless life with a hammer to the skull, one hundred libra iron against an unprotected head.

Flamma fell to the ground.

Lucius watched in horror. The legs Flamma had knocked loose *moved*. Not only that, they *fought*. One of them had caught Flamma and was pinning him down with its claws; the other advanced with open jaws, ready to bite his throat.

Lucius wanted to stop them, wanted to save that big fool, but it all happened so fast. He was too slow.

Kezekem wasn't.

In the blink of an eye, the sciapod had arrived. He kicked the jaw-leg away, but it leaped back to the beast, which rose on now steady legs and roared, once more ready for battle. That was enough for Kezekem to remember that he was no fighter – he wavered, unarmed and frail, and Flamma was still held tight in place by the claw-leg.

Something came shining through the air – Brontes. The lizardwolf slithered between the attacks of the beast, howling and hissing, licking with its venomous tongue. And shot bolts of lightning. Brontes glowed like a storm. Brief flashes of great light in the heavy darkness. Like a thunderstorm on a rainy night. Like Jupiter.

Lucius gaped. *Brontes* was Jupiter's chosen. The one the Vestal had spoken of. It had never been Appia – it was Brontes. Lucius had found her at the Circus, and now, she lit up the darkness of the underground.

Thunderbolt after thunderbolt. The beast burned, and backed away. The leg keeping Flamma in place went up in smoke, and the half-cyclops was free.

The battle wasn't over. Not even Jupiter's chosen, foretold by a sacred Vestal, could defeat the beast. It made another attack. Rushed forward like a bull with all fourteen horns out. Flamma knocked it aside with his sledgehammer, a blow right on its advancing head, but the beast was unharmed.

It seemed so strange. Despite all their dreadful details, all the beats Lucius had seen – both in gladiatorial fights and in papyrus scrolls – had one thing in common; one thing where blemmyes alone were the exception, being controlled by their head. A giant ant couldn't survive without its head, any more than a salamander or a human could. The head was one of the most important aspects of an animal body, and the least protected – vulnerable.

The beast wasn't harmed. Quite the contrary, it only became more furious. Shaking its head, horns intact, tiny golden eyes gleaming underneath. Eyes, mouth, horns – a face, so precious to any animal...

Why did animals have vulnerable heads?

Lucius eyed the beast as it defended itself from the lightning strikes. There it was, that gray slushy belly, bobbing up and down, constantly moving to avoid the lizardwolf's attacks. Puffy and round, with an intricate system of furrows.

"The belly!" he found himself yelling to Flamma.

"Strike its belly! The gray ball! That's its brain!"

Continued dancing, same as before, only now Flamma focused all attacks on the identified target. The beast sent it up and down its body to avoid getting hit; but eventually, Flamma scored a blow, and the belly – the brain – cracked like an egg, splashing over all surroundings.

"Ugh, stench," Flamma said, standing soaked in the gray sludge, and the moment after, Lucius felt it too. A smell as if sprung from the abyss of Tartarus, not merely seeking its way through the nostrils, but pressing sideways over the whole face; like a shell inside the skin, like a mask impossible to remove.

Behind him, he heard Pollio emptying his stomach. And in the sludge that once was the beast, Lucius saw the remains of other animal's carcasses, still not fully digested by the belly that was also a brain or the brain that was also a belly.

"At least now we know what the priests do with the sacrificial leftovers," Lucius said softly.

Kezekem jumped his way over to Flamma, who was scratching the utterly exhausted Brontes with his cyclopic hands. "Good thing you'll be rich soon, amicus. For that tunic's never gonna be clean again."

Flamma looked up, his eyes slowly losing its red glow. "You saved me, Kez. You, Brontes – together."

Kezekem shrugged. "We have a treasure waiting for us."

XXIII

Appia found the whole thing ridiculous. A feast where all of Rome was invited. Dance, exotic animals, gladiators. Despite being practically raised in the Circus, having literally raced in the Circus, she'd only rarely seen gladiators meet their fates in the Circus. There had never been much time for such activities between whipping horses, and being whipped herself.

Ridiculous, but there she was. Truth be told, she didn't have much else to do, and the bread *was* free for the audience. The entertainment too, everything to sell more lottery tickets.

Even though she'd spent her whole life trying to break free – be free – Appia couldn't overcome the gnawing feeling in her chest. She missed her life as a driver.

She didn't see much where she was sitting in the far back, with lots of heads in front of her, and although she was lacking experience in the lion-killing department, she understood how the gladiators felt. The heart pumping so loudly it felt like it was stuck between the ears, the hand aching from gripping the sword, a hundred thousand shouts from the crowds.

So many had chanted her name during her career, that Appia actually was a tad surprised that no one recognized her now, sitting in the middle of their shoves. It seemed Rome housed far too great of a population for it to be possible to keep track of them all.

What little she saw of the games reminded her of Flamma. The one-eyed giant had seemed so innocent, despite his raging violence.

It's tonight, she thought. *Tonight's the night they'll do it.*

An odd feeling, that they would carry out the heist without her, that she had abandoned the creation that she'd been a part of. They had relied on her, and she had betrayed them.

Stop, silly. There's nothing you can do now. It's too late.

Yes, it was too late. And that meant she'd never see her share of the seven hundred thousand denarii Lucius had promised.

Appia shook her head, something she instantly regretted, as her nose briefly went under the armpit of the blemmye sitting next to her; for reasons best left unspoken, the armpit stench of headless creatures was so intense that one would prefer to immediately forget it (which, sadly, was an impossible task, since the smell clung to one's nose for three days minimum). She still doubted that kind of money existed. Who could possibly use all that? Even if she founded her own purple-colored stable at the Circus, importing the best horses in the world, there would still be so much money left that it would form a heap higher than the highest column.

Of course, Lucius had promised that it existed. But that didn't mean anything. Lucius made lots of promises.

Focus on the games, she told herself, pushing her thoughts aside. In the middle of the Circus, a fierce fight still raged in the form of sharpened swords and wild beasts. Bulls charged, lizardwolves surrounded a wounded prey, and fresh giant ants were released to add to the general insanity. An eager kicking-lemur abandoned his fight with a gladiator, rushing to greet the newcomers. With a backflip, he kicked off an ant's head, sending it soaring through the sky.

There was a joint *oh!* from the Circus crowd as the head landed in the front rows, splattering blood; but the audience quickly turned their attention back to the game, watching the kicking-lemur being overwhelmed by the vengeful pack of giant ants.

Appia however, did not. Her eyes were glued to the spot where the head had landed. Right next to it – wiping off ant blood with the back of his hand – sat a man she knew all too well.

Appia felt shivers run down her spine. It was her former master. His eyes turned instantly toward her, ice-cold and grim. Across the entire Circus, his gaze focused directly at her. Crushed her. She lost her breath.

He'll come for me, she realized. *I'm not free. I'm a slave. I'll always be a slave.* The wounds on her back burned, as if they were already preparing to be whipped.

He turned his gaze to the middle of the Circus. Instinctively, Appia followed, seeing the ruckus taking place there.

The dance was over. All gladiators and wild beasts were gone. Only corpses remained. From his box in the lower rows, a figure dressed in toga and holding a shimmering silver staff descended – the Emperor. He would appoint Incitatus to consul.

He stepped into the sand. The cheers of the crowd rose to the sky and beyond. A horse was led in. A gray horse, its mane majestically twisted in braids.

Gray? Appia froze. Incitatus was *black*!
Hostus wasn't there either. There was only one place where he could've gone.

The Emperor discovered the error. He turned around to demand answers, only to find a group of senators and other noblemen. One of them held something small and shiny.

The Emperor was so stunned, that he didn't react until they'd plunged the knife into his heart. They yanked it out and stuck it back in, over and over, leaving his body full of holes. The Praetorian prefect, Clemens, snatched the Emperor's staff.

The crowd had fallen silent.

Then, the screams of terror began.

XXIV

An abyss leading straight to the underground, even though they were already there, darkness below; columns rising from its place, forming a path, wailing in perpetual lamentation at the wind that pulled and pushed like at the top of a mountain.

"It could be a trap," Pollio warned.

"Really?" Lucius said, sweeping the torch in the wind. On every column, hiding behind moss and lichen, a blood-red letter was drawn.

"What does it mean?"

Lucius shook his head. "No idea, but we'll have to solve it before we can pass."

"Perhaps the code we needed to get in?" Pollio suggested. "That thing about socks."

"Hardly. Why use the same password twice? The Treasure of Juno Moneta is worth more than that."

They fell silent and Lucius examined the columns more carefully. Ten rows deep, each with twenty-one letters of the alphabet neatly lined up next to each other. That meant that only the Greek letters Υ and Z were missing; the temple was older than them. So many combinations, only one solution – it reminded him of the lottery.

The little soldier boot rules Rome, but in what socks?

A good idea, coming from Pollio, but no, it couldn't be the answer. For starters, it wasn't ten letters, and even if it was, it would've been too stupid for Lucius' liking. But what *were* ten letters?

"I've got it!" Lucius said.

The others looked at him with raised eyebrows.

"Very simply really, it's *IVNO MONETA*. It's the only ten-letter combination that's logical in the context."

"Juno Moneta?" Kezekem asked, lying on the ground and scratching his chin with his foot. "Ain't that a bit easy?"

"Perhaps," Lucius admitted, "but the answer isn't *IVNO MONETA*, but *MBQR PRQHAD*. You see, I've heard how committed Julius Caesar was to ciphering his letters, a precaution in case the messages fell into the wrong hands; the scrambling followed a shift of three, replacing *A* with *D*. Well, I have reason to believe that the same applies here."

He paused for their objections. But none came. Pollio nodded; Flamma stood with sacks, sledgehammer, and Brontes in his arms; Kezekem brushed fleas from his face. *They're not following, are they? How very surprising.*

"Well," he said, guiding them along, "aren't you going to ask why? Aren't you going to ask why the same rule that the Divine Julius used a hundred years ago applies here? The temple's way older. Aren't you going to ask how these columns are based on his cipher?"

Kezekem yawned. "'Cause this riddle ain't based on Caesar's method, amicus – but vice versa. That's how he seized power, by studying the temple, solving the riddle and harvesting the powers that were hidden here. Then, he let all his letters be a tribute to his source of power, making anyone who figured out his secret words tremble with fear. Anything else?"

"What? How did *you* know that? How!"

"Please amicus, anyone who reads Acta knows that."

"Acta? *Acta Diurna?* Why would I read that rubbish? Nothing but gossip and made-up prophecies! Julius Caesar died one hundred years ago. You weren't even born then!"

"Actually I was," Kezekem said.

"You were?" Lucius narrowed his eyes. "How old are you, anyway?"

Kezekem shrugged. "Older than that dead old geezer."

Lucius rubbed his hands over his face, taking a few deep breaths. He knew sciapods grew older than humans, but not that much older. It seemed strange that Kezekem lived before Rome was ruled by an Emperor, but still bounced around, behaving like a two-year-old.

"And you?" Lucius said to Pollio and Flamma. "By Dis Pater, how did you figure it out?"

Flamma's eye shifted to something pinkish. "Did not figure out. Trust you."

Lucius felt uncomfortable. "It doesn't matter, *MBQR PRQHAD*, that's the way." He paused for effect. "The trap is lethal, and we don't know if my solution is correct. I'd better go first."

No objections.

Bloody cowards, he thought.

He stepped to the edge, took a deep breath and refused to look down. *There's nothing down there*, he told himself, so *there's no reason to look.*

He took a great stride – avoiding, at least, to jump – and found himself standing on the first column, *M*. For a moment, the column shook, as if to set off a trap, and Lucius held his breath as he feared to fall into the abyss. Then, eventually, the column calmed, and he remained in the icy wind.

It could mean that he was right, that the password really was *MBQR PRQHAD*. Or that he'd merely guessed correctly with a one in twenty-one chance. Twenty-one wasn't a particularly large number, even smaller than the twenty-three stab wounds received by Julius Caesar at the day of his murder.

Has the Emperor met the same fate? Lucius thought as he left the column, stepping to the ledge dividing the first and second row. A natural but narrow bridge of stone that allowed Lucius to pick a new column entirely of his own liking. He balanced on the ledge, passing column after column, and found himself standing in front of the second furthest one, *B*.

He took yet another deep breath, and stepped out onto the column. It let him live.

Behind him, his friends cheered, and Lucius himself was so relieved that he almost lost his footing. Then, he remembered that he could still be wrong, be *lucky*, and quickly got nervous again. The probability of guessing correctly twice in a row was one in four hundred forty-one. And that wasn't particularly reassuring, considering four hundred forty-one was even less than the four hundred forty-five days that had formed the Year of Confusion, when Julius Caesar changed the calendar.

Only when the third column didn't protest did Lucius really feel true joy bubbling up his belly. Three in a row! What was the probability of that? One in nine thousand two hundred sixty-one! That was equal to... to... eh! That's all he knew of Julius Caesar.

He practically danced across the last seven columns.

On the other side, the world once more narrowed to the shape of a tunnel. The entrance was marked by a gate carved from the mountain, adorned with winding decorations of gods and beasts and demons that seemed to come alive as the red glow of the torch smiled upon them. Was that where the treasure hid? Dis Pater, something glittered in there!

Lucius took two quick steps before halting. He shouldn't find the treasure alone. It wouldn't be right. The others were just as much a part of this as he was, they deserved to share the triumph. And who knew what beasts awaited yet? Probably best that Flamma came along. Lucius turned slowly, begrudgingly, and looked back the way he'd come. The others were nowhere to be seen. The light of the torch was growing weaker, barely reaching across the abyss.

"Hey!" he shouted. "Do you hear me?"

His echo replied, but nothing more. A searing shiver ran through his body. *We've been discovered. The Praetorians have captured them. I'm all alone.*

"Loud and clear!" Pollio's voice answered from the darkness. "And we see your little dot of light over there, like a star!"

"Come here, then! Just remember: *M-B-Q-R-P-R-Q-H-A-D!*"

"But Lucius, we can't!"

Can't? Lucius thought. *What do you mean can't?* Then it hit him. *The darkness. They can't see.*

"I'll come back!" he shouted.

MBQR PRQHAD, he thought, and started walking.

***

Pollio stood with his mouth wide open as Lucius returned.

"Hungry?" Lucius queried.

Pollio blinked, as if broken from a spell. "You came from *there!*" he said, pointing to a column.

"Yeah?"

"And you left *that way!*" Pollio said, pointing in another direction. "First on *M* and now on *D!*"

Lucius felt his heart sink, as if he'd lost it in the abyss. *He's right. I followed the same password in both directions – that is reverse and different paths. But that means…*

"I'm sorry," he said, "but we never did figure out the

password."

*****

Flamma didn't seem convinced. "Trap is not falling down? Trap is getting to other side?"

"Yes, I saw a room there. I thought it was the treasure chamber, but now I understand it's a prison. Whatever's in the abyss — that's where we're going."

"Right amicus," Kezekem said casually, "let's have a go at it then. Ain't nothing gonna happen if we guess wrong."

Lucius sighed. "Do you know how many combinations there are? You live long, apparently, but you'd still never finish in your lifetime. If everything went according to the Plan, the Emperor is dead now, but even that won't make us invisible forever."

They tried anyway. Flamma gently put Brontes down, the animal still being completely exhausted, and borrowed the torch to try a seemingly random combination. It didn't work. Kezekem ignored the columns, instead jumping on the ledges between them — on his way back he took his single leg and walked right in the middle, forming an *LLLLLLLLLL*, but to no avail.

"I hope you're gonna try something clever," Pollio said after testing an unciphered *IVNO MONETA*.

"I've already tried, as you know," Lucius said.

"But you will try again."

"No," Lucius said, spitting. "I won't try again. I've told you, there's no use. You would've realized that too if you weren't so bloody stupid. We lost. We'll never reach the treasure."

Pollio backed off. He sat down on the ground with Flamma and Kezekem, all three casting sideways glances at Lucius. They seemed upset that Lucius was upset, but he had every right to be. He'd put his heart into the Plan. Held it in his mind every waking moment, relating everything he saw to it: a potential crew member there, a potential enemy there, a thought, a scent, a day.

All for nothing. There wouldn't be any seven hundred sixty-three thousand denarii, there wouldn't be anything at all. And it was his own fault. They hadn't lost because some beast had beaten Flamma, or because Kezekem had failed to shadow a Praetorian. They'd lost because Lucius couldn't crack a code. He should've been able to; he had freed a gladiator, tricked Clemens into believing an ordinary stone had magical powers, wriggled his way past the priest and...

Wait, what did the priest say? *The little soldier boot rules Rome, but in what socks?* Pollio had suggested it, but it didn't consist of ten letters. What it did consist of, however, were ten words.

The little soldier boot rules Rome, but in what socks? T-L-S-B-R-R-B-I-V-S.

It may not be right – no, probably wrong – but it was worth a shot. And if it didn't work, Lucius would jump into the abyss.

***

Lucius passed the column before turning to the others, lighting their way. The tightly wrapped pieces of cloth at the end of the torch had grown increasingly thin, and Lucius feared it wasn't long before it would burn out. The ledge became dangerously crowded, but they managed to reach the next column without falling to a very painful death.

What if there is no treasure, Lucius thought as they walked. It seemed unlikely, but the disguised prison on the other side of the abyss had Lucius thinking. He remembered something Appia had said when he'd presented the Plan: *That much money doesn't exist.*

Why would Lucius believe in the huge sums Green Gnaeus promised to the winner of his lottery? Why would the green-clad leprechaun pay anything at all? Perhaps that's why no one ever won, because there was nothing to win.

An unpleasant thought – he forced himself to focus on the riddle instead. "Last column, *S*."

Lucius stepped on it, preparing to sink into the abyss, where the treasure surely await. But nothing happened. He was on the other side. Another failed attempt. The riddle was still unsolved. The others crossed as well; no one sunk into the abyss.

But the mountain wall in front of them opened with a crack.

There, next to the gate Lucius had seen earlier, was an additional gate. Identical to the first. Gods and beasts and demons that came alive.

"Incredible," Lucius mumbled, walking up to the new gate.

"Holy powers," Flamma said. "*T'rrch'un* guide us."

"Pollio," Lucius said, "you stay here and keep watch. We'd better not get surprised in there, with all that gold in our hands; not now when the riddle of the columns is solved. Warn us if anyone comes."

"How?" Pollio asked with a voice that made Lucius feel guilty.

"With your flute, of course. Its atrocious tones are impossible to miss."

Pollio nodded. It was an indisputable fact.

"Flamma, you can leave Brontes with Pollio. Saves you the trouble of carrying her."

The half-cyclops shook his head. "Brontes with me. Always."

Lucius held the torch through the gate. A passage appeared there, narrower than before. "Well, let's go then."

XXV

"There yet?" Flamma asked. He walked with both back and knees bent, Brontes and sacks in his arms, his sledgehammer pressed against his body with his elbow.

Lucius glanced behind his back. They'd left the entrance both far behind and far above them. "Yes," he replied, in an equal attempt to comfort himself as Flamma. "We're almost there."

Shortly after, the passage widened, and a new cavern lay before them.

"There it is!" Kezekem exclaimed, dashing off.

Dis Pater, Lucius thought, *so much for sharing the triumph.*

Kezekem squealed. Ice-cold and ghastly.

"That's no cry of joy," Lucius said, running after him with Flamma.

Kezekem lay on the ground, shaking. Above him rose a shadow, dark red – a monster so terrifying that Lucius fell to the ground. He felt sick.

Flamma dropped Brontes and rushed forward, swinging his hammer. Useless. Passing through the monster without a sound.

Lucius tried to get up but the world spun. He looked at the monster, a deep red shadow with a tiny figure inside. It made no sound. Was quiet as ashes. Like death or nothing.

Brontes, Lucius thought weakly, *Jupiter's chosen. Wake up, save us.* But the lizardwolf lay with her tongue out, tail tucked under her body, knocked out from exhaustion. From her no help would come.

Lucius leaned on the torch and managed to get on his feet, breathing in gasps. His legs gave way, but he wobbled to a halt and remained standing. He had to defeat the monster himself. Try, anyway. He stumbled forward.

Flamma made another attack. Spun around with his hammer. The shadow swept away, and the hammer shattered. Still, utter, impermeable silence.

Lucius' torch died out. He stumbled and fell back to the ground. Seeing nothing, hearing nothing; feeling too much.

A sound broke through. The terrible cry of the monster. No, worse. Much, *much* worse. Pollio played the flute.

The monster exploded in a flurry of glowing red flakes. Everything came visible, Kezekem endlessly shaking, Flamma holding shards of his hammer; Pollio, flute in hand.

Lucius sat up. "How…" he began, cutting off when he got flakes on his tongue; they filled his whole mouth with a sucking, bitter taste, and he coughed to expel them. "How'd you know? That the shadow couldn't stand noise?"

Pollio shook his head. "I didn't. I came to warn you. Green Gnaeus is here. He appeared out of nowhere. Went straight to the other gate, without seeing me. I didn't want him to hear me, so I hurried down here."

"Green Gnaeus?" Lucius didn't understand. Did he always feel this confused? "Green Gnaeus can't be here. Kezekem said he was at the Circus."

Kezekem said… by Dis Pater! He crawled over to the sciapod. "Wake up," he said, poking Kezekem, "you have to wake up."

Kezekem continued to shake. His eyes were wide open, although he saw nothing.

"He gone," Flamma said. "Never return."

Lucius grew cold. Kezekem… gone? He couldn't believe it. Kezekem stared with eyes that had never seen the sun. That would never see the sun. Eyes that…

Kezekem gasped and regained consciousness.

Alive. Of course he was alive. Since when was *Flamma* a medical expert.

Lucius pushed his feelings aside. There was no time for such things. They had a heist to take care of, and Green Gnaeus had come to stop them. "You lied. You said Green Gnaeus was holding a lottery, but he's here now, so that's impossible. Why Kezekem? Why must you always lie?"

"Okay, amicus, I'll sit," Kezekem whispered, sitting up. The fleas fell from his face, dead and burned. "And I spoke the truth too. I always do, you know that. Just think, why would the leprechaun miss a chance to make some big coins? It's been a long time since the Circus was that packed. 'Course he held a lottery."

"He was lugging a big sack," Pollio added. "I think he was going to drop off his earnings of the day."

The Gods, they're right. Green Gnaeus comes here after every lottery, dropping off the bets. And why would he fight his way past his monsters? Why would he jump on columns where his legs are too short to walk? He has a shortcut.

"We've moved quite a bit from the temple, here in the underground," Lucius said, "and I believe we're right under the Circus now. Somehow, Green Gnaeus has made his way straight down here."

They fell silent, turning their heads to the ground above, listening for the cheers and shouts of the crowd. Nothing reached their ears.

"What now, amicus?" Kezekem said, seemingly feeling better from talking.

"Now we win Green Gnaeus' lottery."

***

They fumbled their way back in blind. In such complete darkness that the narrowness of the passage suddenly felt like something positive, seeing how it eliminated the risk of getting lost. Or diminished it, anyway; Lucius no longer knew what to think of the laws of nature that ruled in the underground of Juno Moneta.

Regardless, they found their way back to where Pollio had been keeping watch. Where they had chosen the wrong gate. A gust of wind greeted them as the abyss welcomed them back.

A green glow shone from the other gate. Lucius nodded toward it, and they sneaked closer. The glow was enough for Lucius to signal with his hands.

Flamma put Brontes down, clenching the fist where he'd previously held his sledgehammer; Kezekem leaned forward, ready to pounce; Pollio held his flute tightly in hand – he'd use it as a blunt instrument rather than an *instrument* instrument.

"Now," Lucius whispered, and they rushed in.

The light originated from Green Gnaeus' lantern, which emitted luminous green smoke. Green Gnaeus shone straight at them, and Lucius' eyes stung and burned and teared.

"Ye intruders, halt!" Green Gnaeus the Great and Greedy roared, his voice both strangely squeaky and mighty low. "Walk no closer to the treasure that be not yers!"

They obeyed, oddly enough. The plan had been to take the leprechaun by surprise, not be thwarted by his words. Very well, they were discovered, might as well listen to what he had to say.

Slowly, Lucius grew accustomed to the smoke light. And by Dis Pater, what a sight he faced! The leprechaun stood in his mysterious green clothes, his hat, his flame-colored beard, atop a mountain, an Olympus of coins: gold, silver, copper, electrum, aurichalcum, and bronze. He shone like he himself was Juno Moneta. The treasure *was*, and it was magnificent.

"Yer not worthy of Monetas' treasure, ye can't be robbin' her."

"But it's not Moneta we rob," Lucius said. "It's you. Or, no, it's you who robs Rome. We've come to put an end to that."

Green Gnaeus laughed. He moved his mouth back and forth in a spasmodic grimace, spewing lengthy, hissing *HA-HA-HA*s, as if trying to get rid of something stuck in his throat.

"I've stolen nothin'. Rome plays fer Rome wants to play, and I be helpin' her. But enough o' that. Well done fer comin' this far, nobody ever be comin' this far before, but now yers journey be endin'. Turn 'round, ye buggers, an' I'll not be callin' fer Crimsonus."

"Crimsonus?" Lucius said. "You mean that silent monster? The red shadow? It's dead."

"Dead?" Something strange swept across Green Gnaeus' face, his eyes sank deeper into their sockets, his beard darkened, his brow furrowed. It lasted but a fleeting moment before his face returned to its normal state. Perhaps it was nothing more than the green smoke of the lantern playing tricks in the shadows. "Liar! Crimsonus ain't be dead! Crimsonus never be dead! Ye cannot be killin' him, ye've never met him!"

"Of course we have," Lucius said and took a step forward, feeling more confident, "we went down. We took the other gate and met him. Just like you planned. I'll admit it was a tricky move, that the correct gate requires no password; that the gate to the treasure, the gate leading to *here*, was open all along."

Green Gnaeus laughed again. It made Lucius uneasy. "Yer sayin' that, *HA-HA-HA*, that ye passed through Crimsonus' gate! The one openin' every night at sunset! *HA-HA-HA*, so ye went in, *HA-HA-HA*! Ye went in an' killed him."

Green Gnaeus' laughter was tears.

Dis, Lucius thought, *the columns were merely a deterrent. There was no password, no riddle to crack. We just happened to arrive at the right time.*

"Ye be not understandin'!" Green Gnaeus yelled, beating his chest, crying. "Ye be not understandin'. Crimsonus be *me*. Me good side. Defendin' what be existin', protectin'. Ye've killed me good side! What be left o' me now? The bad, only the bad. The one who be collectin', the one who be makin' profit from others. Ye've destroyed me."

Green Gnaeus the Great and Greedy fell from his mountain. He lay on the ground, lantern beside him, sobbing his green little heart out.

Kezekem jumped past him. He began scraping up coins for one of the sacks Flamma had brought. "Amici, give me a hand will you!"

"But what about Green Gnaeus?" Pollio said. "What should we do with him?"

"Eh, never mind the weeprechaun. He's just lying there. Come on and get packing."

"Kezekem's right," Lucius agreed, "the sooner we get out of here, the better."

As soon as Kezekem had stuffed his sack, he threw it over his shoulder, snatched Green Gnaeus' lantern and leapt off in full speed, same way they'd come. Lucius glanced after the sciapod as he disappeared in a cloud of glowing green smoke, and for a moment he wondered if he'd made a terrible mistake. Kezekem could slip away, a single sack would be more than enough for a life of luxury. He'd taken the lantern, and even if the smoke still lingered, it wouldn't be long before it vanished, leaving them blind in the dark.

Now you doubt him? After everything he's done? The thought made Lucius sick, but to be fair, he'd only known the sciapod for a few days. Well, it couldn't be helped, the mountain must be moved. Kezekem was the only one quick enough for the job.

Quick indeed. Lucius had barely finished his thought before the sciapod returned with the look of someone who'd packed a sack of coins at the hiding place above ground and wondered why no one had prepared the next sack for him.

"How'd it go?" Lucius asked. "Any guards up in the temple?"

"Not a single one, amicus. I peeked outside the temple and the city is in full riot. People run around like crazy, screaming that the Emperor is dead. And the city ain't nothing but a big fire, with flames hungry like a hungry, fiery, flame thing."

Lucius frowned, again wondering if this creature really was some hundred plus years old.

"Come on now, amicus – the sack, gimme the sack."

He got a sack and disappeared. Lucius and Pollio stuffed one after another, placed them on the ground, and Kezekem appeared out of nowhere to pick them up. Flamma was watching Green Gnaeus, ensuring that the leprechaun didn't try any tricks.

More than ninety sacks they'd smuggled as Flammas bandage, and stuffing them should've been hard work, considering the sheer weight of their content – but never had Lucius felt so easy in body and mind. His hands worked of their own accord, never resting, and with every coin his finger crossed, with every little emperor he squashed with his thumb, his mouth drew itself ever higher with a force he couldn't possibly restrain. Olympus shrunk to an everyday mountain, and then to a hill, to a knoll, to a knob, and to nothing.

"Don't bother," Lucius said as Kezekem moved to one of the four remaining sacks. "We'll take one each on our way back."

"What about him?" Kezekem asked, pointing toward Green Gnaeus. "I bet he got something tucked away in his hat. Look how big it is."

"No bets please," Lucius muttered, but Flamma lifted the leprechaun by his feet, shaking him up and down. The only thing falling to the ground was a yellow, crumpled lottery ticket. Not even Green Gnaeus was immune to his game.

Kezekem laughed as a red-faced Green Gnaeus flapped his arms to break free from the cyclops that to him wasn't merely half.

"Stop!" Pollio said. "Stop it!"

"Why upset?" Flamma queried, but set Greene Gnaeus down.

"Why? Only savages shake people like that. If you wish to be a savage, by all means carry on."

Hesitantly, Flamma lifted Green Gnaeus again.

"But amicus, we gotta do something 'bout him," Kezekem insisted. "Leprechauns are liars, everyone knows that."

Flamma nodded in agreement. "Most safe, kill him."

"We're not doing that," Lucius said.

Flamma shrugged.

"Nah-huh, but we can't trust him," Kezekem continued.

"Let me join ye!" Green Gnaeus whined. "Me bad side be all that's left o' me, let me join ye! I be pleadin' with ye, please, ye bad lot be all the hope I got!"

It went quiet. It was a strange plea Green Gnaeus made, to join his robbers, his destroyers. Lucius didn't know what to think.

"We have to do it," Pollio eventually said. "Because we are good, because we are evil – I don't know. But we've annihilated him. The least we can do is to grant him this. We'll take him above ground, to the temple, and leave his fate in Moneta's hands."

Flamma shook his head in a way that made his eye twirl, and Kezekem said, "Nah amicus, it won't do. Bad idea I tell you."

Oh, Dis Pater, why am I doing this, Lucius thought, and said, "It *will* do. Pollio has better judgment than us in these matters, and the Bane of Crimsonus deserves our trust."

They did as told. One sack each over their shoulders, Brontes once more on wobbly slithering paws, Green Gnaeus walking between them. To escape the insufferable weeping of the leprechaun, they'd given back his lantern, and he already appeared to be in a better mood as he whistlingly led the party through his green, mint-scented smoke.

"Doesn't he seem a bit too happy, amicus?" Kezekem whispered in Lucius' ear as they walked. "A moment ago he cried like he wanted to challenge the Tiber. He's up to something, I swear."

Lucius nodded. "Perhaps, but this is the best way to keep an eye on him."

"That's why my task," Flamma said, voice filled with pride. "You – two eyes."

They reached the Abyss of the Columns, and its wind tore and pulled the smoke they brought. To his surprise, Lucius saw how their new guide did a sharp turn away from the columns.

"What are you doing?"

"He's trying to stall," Kezekem said sourly. "I'm telling you, amicus, we can't trust him. He's doing everything he can to delay us just enough for the Praetorians to stop us. Slow us down."

"Stall?" Green Gnaeus said as if the accusation hurt him more than the usage of uncontracted words. "No I ain't! It be the opposite. I'm only helpin'. Showin' the quickest way up, that's all."

"Is that your way?" Lucius asked with a slight nod in the direction Green Gnaeus had been heading. "The one leading to the Circus?"

"Aye, it be the best way. Listen to me words."

"I believe," Lucius said, "that it's the best way to go straight to the lion's den. The Circus is the last place we want to be right now – we're not so stupid as to let you lead us there." Green Gnaeus sighed. "The hard way it be, then."

As they were passing the first column, Flamma took Green Gnaeus under his arm, carrying him like a handless amphora. "How kind of ye," Green Gnaeus muttered from Flamma's armpit. "Afraid I'll be fallin'?"

"A safety measure," Lucius explained, "It'd be a real shame if we were left all by ourselves."

Flamma took good care of his captive at every column they passed. But when they stepped to the fifth column, right above the abyss, Green Gnaeus hissed a terrible laugh. He dropped his lantern and it clanged against a column before disappearing into the darkness.

"You…" Flamma began, but was interrupted by a kick to his chest that almost made him lose his balance.

Green Gnaeus lunged against Lucius with a roar. Lucius had no time to react. Nowhere to go. The little monster would hit him, drag him to his death.

Green Gnaeus was stopped by a clink.

For a brief moment, he was stuck midair. Frozen, with a surprised look on his face and a warm hug around the sack of coins. Then, Green Gnaeus – regarded as great by few, as greedy by most, as the rightful goose king by that madman in south Suburra who thought everyone but him were birds – dropped down and disappeared.

"Pollio," the now sackless Kezekem said after a moment's silence "that's from your share."

"What? Mine? But there were over eight thousand denarii in there!"

Lucius took a deep breath, and carefully sat down on the ledge. He felt giddy. Around him, the wind howled as the remaining smoke from the lantern was devoured by the abyss.

"We can take it from my share," he said, as the darkness grew heavier, "but only if you find a way to get us out of here."

XXVI

Their eyes never did adapt to the dark.

"I'll jump," Kezekem eventually announced, "jump and hope for the best. It was alright before, with the lantern, I know the distances now. And I'll return with light."

Lucius shook his head, forgetting that no one could see him. "You're dead if you jump."

"What about Brontes?" Pollio said. "She's back on her feet. Those thunderbolts she shot before, can't she do that again?"

"She too weak," Flamma said in a rumbling voice. "What she did – special. Link with cinnamon birds. Heard of such things."

Brontes hissed in her yaps. She didn't seem to appreciate being called weak.

"Amicus," Kezekem said, "I've *gotta* go back up. The gold… I hid it well, I swear I did, but it's so much. Someone will find it."

He was right. The hiding place was the storeroom in the temple where the *victimarius* kept his axe and other tools. A decent temporary hiding place, but all it took was one glance at the glittering treasure inside, and your eyes suffered from life-long impairment. The *victimarius* wouldn't be there until the daily ceremony, but considering the riot that had struck the city, Lucius wouldn't be surprised if the demand for axes had risen to the point where people lost all respect for the sanctity of the temple.

"Look!" Pollio said.

"Where?" Lucius turned his head. Still, he saw nothing but darkness.

"There! Right over there! Toward the temple!"

Lucius squinted at the direction – at least what he thought was at the direction – and saw a faint flicker. It disappeared, but then reappeared. A little dot, yellow and wonderful.

By Dis Pater! A torch! Who could it be? Someone wondering where Green Gnaeus had gone? Or a priest who'd discover that everything wasn't as it should? They needed the light, but perhaps it was best to—

"*HELLOOO!*" Flamma bellowed through the darkness.

Stupid half-cyclops, Lucius thought as he saw the light grow steadier.

A brittle voice answered them. "H-hey, mister Turpilinus? It's me. H-Hostus."

Hostus? Lucius thought. *What's he doing down here?*

"Yes, I'm here," Lucius said. "And you must be our savior. Get over here with the torch, will you?"

"H-here? Where's that?"

"That would be in the middle of the bottomless abyss of death, on top of the columns painted with ominous letters written in blood."

Lucius could almost hear Hostus gulping across the abyss. He smiled. "Don't worry. It's not a trap. You shouldn't fall down as long as you watch where you put your feet. And it's not blood. I think."

"Are you sure we can trust him?" Kezekem said quietly.

"He's a part of our crew."

"He is?"

Lucius' smile widened. "He is now."

***

"How'd you know we were here?" Lucius asked as they hurried from the abyss back to the temple.

"I waited outside," Hostus said, who'd calmed down and spoke more clearly, "like you told me to. But I thought things were taking too long, so when the Praetorian left his post, I snuck into the temple. I saw the shadowfoot tucking away a sack in some room, and then disappearing down the trapdoor again. But by Incitatus he's quick! I couldn't say anything before he was gone, so I stood there, waiting. When no one came I was worried, so I followed his track. The trapdoor was open, after all."

"You left the trapdoor open?" Lucius asked Kezekem, who jumped by his side. "Are you out of your mind? Someone could've noticed!"

Kezekem threw out his arms. "D'you know how much time it takes to pull that lever? I ain't have time for that, amicus, and it's a good thing someone noticed."

Lucius rolled his eyes, but rather than answering, he covered his nose; they'd reached the place where they had fought the beast with a belly as a brain. The gray slush which they trod in still emitted a heavy stench. They scurried by. The well awaited them, torches on the wall. A ladder leading up from the underground.

***

The treasure was untouched, thank gods.

"Hostus," Lucius said, "where did you leave the

chariot?"

"In one of the buildings next door, as per instructions."

"Good, bring it to the temple gate. I want this to go as smoothly as possible."

Hostus hurried off. When he opened the gate, the sounds of the riotous city drifted into the temple.

"Alright, final act," Lucius said. "Time to end this."

Flamma and Brontes posted up at the gate to frighten off any curious eyes. "Here now!" Flamma yelled shortly after.

Lucius was out of breath already by the first time he ran from the storeroom to the chariot. There they were, eight horses eagerly stomping their hooves in the night, including the black beast who'd come so close to consulship.

Lucius turned to fetch another sack, but Kezekem had already taken care of it. Everything was packed, the chariot slumping under the weight. Time to go. Lucius climbed into the chariot, sitting behind Hostus on the wonderfully uncomfortable sacks of coins. The rest of the crew squeezed up beside him as Hostus gripped his whip tightly and prepared to lash.

"Stop right there, criminal scum!"

Behind them, from the temple, a figure emerged. A dwarf in shining armor and a buckled helmet with a yellow plume. He looked like a rooster.

"Dwarf," Flamma grunted. "I *hate* dwarves."

"Not just any dwarf. I'm Thrakatulus, *praefectus vigilum*. We've met earlier, as you may recall?"

"What do you want from us?" Lucius said. "Stop us from leaving with the loot? Please, it's no concern of yours. I killed the Emperor to whom you felt such hatred; you can go back to hunting salamanders. They seem active tonight."

One of Thrakatulus' eyes twitched, and he spoke in a lisping manner. "If his death truly is your doing, I applaud you, you kept your word. But then, allow me to do the same. I want the giant. He's my convict, and he fled. And I want you. You too swore the gladiator's oath. You too are a convict. You too are a runaway slave."

Lucius bit his skin under his nails and studied the prefect.

He'd been annoyed when Pollio had reported that it was the Praetorians and not the Vigiles who were their hunters following the freeing of Flamma, but maybe the Vigiles weren't as incompetent as he'd assumed. Thrakatulus was the one who'd found them, not Clemens.

"How did you know?" Lucius said, removing his fingers from his mouth. "How did you know about our heist?"

"A priest came to me, babbling something about Juno Moneta's geese warning him that a Gaul was attacking his temple. I didn't understand half of his ramblings, but then he showed me the cuts on his wrists. The intruders had tied him up. But he'd gotten loose, and I came right away."

How could I be so stupid? Lucius thought, feeling the rage growing inside. Not only had he tied the priest far too loose, but when they walked by, Lucius hadn't even noticed he was gone!

"Forget about the dwarf," Kezekem said. "We gotta go, amicus, he ain't stopping us now."

For once, Kezekem was right. Lucius' mistake had led them to be found; he was not going to let it lead to them also being bound. He turned to Hostus, to where the driver was sitting, and asked him to whip his horses. Whip them harder than he'd ever done before.

But Hostus wasn't there. He lay with his face shoved to the ground. A dwarf sat with his knee on his back, gladius to his neck; somehow, the dwarf had climbed onto the chariot without being noticed, and tackled the driver. Hostus squealed to be released.

"I hope you didn't think I went to all this trouble just to bid you farewell?" Thrakatulus snapped his fingers, and suddenly they were surrounded by fifty dwarves.

Flamma made a move to jump down, but Lucius gripped his massive arm and managed to stop him with a look. Had they been at the Circus, Flamma could've given them a fight, possibly even won despite missing a weapon, but here, where he had to protect not only himself but also his friends and his gold, he stood no chance. Lucius was glad Flamma understood.

"If the giant jumps," Thrakatulus said, to make matters even more clear, "your driver no longer has a head."

"*He's* not their driver."

Lucius turned his head, feeling blood rushing through his veins. That sounded like...

Appia dashed forward. The ring of dwarves was facing the chariot. Excellent for stopping those who wanted out, worse for stopping those who wanted in. She darted between the dwarves, spinning and dodging their blows with ease, and climbed into the chariot. Sat down on the driver's seat.

"I didn't want to miss the big day," she said in response to her friend's fallen jaws.

Lucius gathered himself. Appia was back! Great, they could leave, they could escape, but Hostus...

He looked at the driver. Hostus still lay pressed to the ground, dwarf above him; it almost looked comical, like he had been defeated by a child. Hostus had only been a part of the crew for a short while, but Lucius couldn't leave him like that. Leave him to die.

Appia must've seen what he was thinking. "Lucius, leave him. He meant to betray us from the start. He's here on Clemens' behalf."

Clemens? So Hostus was a risk after all! How did Appia know? He shook his head. It didn't matter how she knew. Hostus was the enemy. He gladly left the enemy.

"No!" Hostus cried from the ground, into the ground,

pounding the ground. "You c-can't leave without me. You c-can't take Incitatus from me! Oh, Incitatus, my beautiful h-h… my beautiful unicorn!"

"*Unicorn?*" Appia said. She stared at Incitatus, at Hostus, at Incitatus again. Then she laughed. "That explains a lot. But surely a unicorn can muscle through some dwarves."

She flicked her whip, and the horses and unicorn took off. Cowardly dwarves threw themselves away, brave dwarves were butted by Incitatus' hornless head. They were free.

"Let go!" Hostus barked behind them. "Let go, you idiots! Y-you've ruined everything! After them! Seize them!"

The world flew by. Appia led them down the slopes of Capitoline Hill, through angry crowds and battered senators, over roaring fires, and through a city in chaos. Straight past the Circus Maximus, and out through the Servian Wall. Away. Leaving the city behind. With sacks brimming with coins of all sorts and more at that.

They were immortal.

XXVII

The screams still echoed in Clemens' ears. The smell of blood lingered in his nose, the smell of fear. He squeezed the Jadecrystal so hard that his hand went numb.

It couldn't have been more than a few hours since the Emperor's death, but it seemed longer than the four years Clemens had been a prefect. Time felt slower with the Jadecrystal. Perhaps it was.

He had ripped it right out of the scepter. The others had been too focused on the Emperor to care, but Clemens' eyes had been solely fixed on the green, shimmering stone. It had given him a jolt, and he'd felt energy surge inside of him.

By then, the Emperor had already been coughing blood. When it was Clemens' turn, the Emperor could barely stand, but some kind of life still hid in those ghastly gray-blue eyes – Clemens chose to believe that it was his stab that finally killed it. He had pulled the knife out of the Emperor's stomach and made a new hole next to the others.

Oathbreaker, he thought, *that's what I am*. It made him feel proud.

Most of the audience had left the Circus. To hide in the city. To destroy it. But a few remained, staring at the dead body glistening in the moonlight. Paralyzed by the corpse much like

Clemens was paralyzed by the Jadecrystal.

"I wish it had been me."

Clemens turned to see who'd uttered the words. When he saw it was the blemmye and ex-consul Valerius Asiaticus, he was surprised. "That was killed instead of your Emperor? But you hate him."

"Epona no!" Asiaticus said and laughed. "I mean that I wish it had been me who slayed him. Today was a big day. Rome will never be the same."

Clemmens nodded. That might be true, but why did Asiaticus speak of it? Why did he linger at the Circus?

"I'm counting on your support," Asiaticus explained. "Rome will need someone new to rule her. I'll treat the Praetorians well if you support me."

A blemmye as emperor? It seemed absurd. But there was a peaceful dignity to Asiaticus as he left the Circus, his toga pristine, stepping into the burning city. Clemens knew he should follow. Lead his Praetorians to order, and save the city from itself. He knew, he even wanted to, but he couldn't. Not until he'd punished those damned Gladiator Thieves.

Where was Hostus? The driver had said it would happen in the evening, but the night had already marched far along on its path. The Praetorians Clemens had managed to detain in order to deal with the thieves were growing restless; they wouldn't stay put much longer.

Then, finally, Hostus arrived, galloping through the gates of the Circus, swift as the Ceryneian hind, and on a horse barely visible behind all its foam.

On a horse. Not a unicorn. Not with a chariot of Gladiator Thieves.

Clemens met him, and Hostus dismounted as the horse collapsed. "The thieves, they got away. And with so much gold. I was told in advance, the location, the heist. I didn't tell you.

Y-you were so busy, and I thought, doesn't matter if y-you know, I'll take the thieves h-here anyway, no need to c-come there. J-juno Moneta, her temple, they robbed her temple!"

Clemens' hearts beat out of sync. They had escaped, they had slipped out of his grip. And they had robbed the Temple of Juno Moneta.

The Temple of Juno Moneta! By Saturn, they have robbed the Temple of Juno Moneta!

"It wasn't my fault," Hostus continued. "It was going so well, but then they c-came from nowhere and stopped me. They…" He saw the Emperor and fell silent. His eyes grew wide, and in a brief gesture he pinched his nose. The stench must've reached him. As if to hide it, he dipped his hand in the puddle of sweat on his forehead.

"Who?" Clemens demanded. "Companions? Any we still can catch?"

Hostus pulled his gaze from the corpse and shook his head. "The Vigiles. They took me h-h… they took me hostage. But Turpilinus, h-he ignored me. Left me. Left me to die."

Of course he did – he's a criminal. What did the Vigiles think, that he would just give up his treasure?

Hostus couldn't say where they fled, but he did manage to leave descriptions of the thieves. These, however, proved to be of little use than confirming what was already known from the Gladiator Theft: their leader had a wart on his forehead, the gladiator was the famous half-cyclops, the shadowfoot was incomprehensibly quick.

The shadowfoot's appearance? Round teeth. Oh, that certainly narrowed it down, anything else? They'd brought along a flutist as entertainment. And more? The half-cyclops had a pet lizardwolf he raised and bathed and probably named.

Madmen, Clemens thought.

"Names? For the thieves, that is."

Hostus contemplated this, calming his breathing in the process. "Don't know, we didn't exchange salutations. But the leader's name is Lucius Turpilinus. And..." He trailed off, staring at the ground.

"What?"

Hostus looked up, biting his lip. "And I recognized one of them. Appia, a driver for the Whites. The best."

Clemens raised his eyebrows. Appia, that was the young woman he had seen when he'd questioned the White Team's trainer. He hadn't thought she had it in her.

That was all Hostus had to say. The Gladiator Thieves had escaped. The Gladiator Thieves had robbed the Temple of Juno Moneta.

XXVIII

"How'd you know?" a voice said. Appia took her eyes off the road and saw that Lucius had climbed up to her side.

"Know what?" Appia said, whipping Incitatus. Even though they had slowed down, the unicorn dragged so hard that she had a great deal of trouble keeping him under control.

"Know that Hostus was working for Clemens? That he would betray us?"

"I…" *Come on, stop being so silly.* "After we met when you gave me that sack of food at the Forum, I followed you. I think I was hoping, deep down, that you would confront me again. It was as if I never quite thought you would just let me go. But then I saw you meet Hostus – you traded me for Hostus! You should know how angry I was – at you, at Hostus, at myself. How could I have done what I did, betraying those who'd put their trust in me? Hostus was in such a hurry after seeing you that I had to figure out what was going on. I've probably never run that fast before, but I managed to follow him to Suburra. He rushed into an insula, and I hid in the opposite room to listen."

Lucius laughed. "In the opposite room? What did you think of it?"

Laughter? What was so funny about that? She didn't think the story was something to laugh about.

"Sorry," Lucius eventually said, "what did he have to say?"

"Hostus? That you had a wart on your forehead. Clemens was harder to hear, not the same squeaky tone of voice."

Lucius ran his fingers through his hair, sweeping down a lock. "Hey, we need a rest. We've been riding for hours. Pull over and stop over there."

"You know, you look kind of silly in that priest-toga," Appia said while stopping the horses. Incitatus wasn't very keen on it, but she managed to bend him to her will.

Lucius dragged at the strings of his toga; it was dirty and ripped into pieces from his adventures underground. "I haven't had the time to change. But it looks pretty good now, doesn't it? Like a thief-toga."

"We can't stop here," Pollio said, apparently uninterested in discussions on fashion. "We have to keep going. What if they come for us?"

"Relax. We should be in Tarracina soon. Rome is far behind us."

There was a deep pond, glimmering in the first light of the day. Appia led the horses there to drink. They didn't bother to make a fire, but instead sat down around the ashes of fires that once burned.

A group of noblemen rode past them. Appia held her breath, but they showed no interest in them. Just as no one had done. People probably assumed they were farmers, slightly more common for your sacks to be filled with wheat than with gold.

"Ain't it great?" Kezekem said, lying in the shade of his foot, twirling a big gold coin between his fingers. "We did it. We actually did it."

Pollio nodded, as in relief, and Flamma petted Brontes.

Yes, Appia thought, *we did it. I'm free and have more than I ever imagined.*

"We may have scored the jackpot, but we're not done yet," Lucius warned. "Remember, we need to cross the entire Mare Nostrum. And besides…"

"What?" Pollio asked.

Lucius shook his head. He stared into the dormant firepit. "Nothing. Just a feeling. Like I've forgotten something."

Kezekem threw the coin right in Lucius' face. "Amicus, why so boring all of a sudden, eh? Everything's here, enjoy it!"

Appia wanted to agree with Kezekem, she really wanted to. She wanted to be happy. "Don't you feel the slightest bit bad about it?" she asked instead. "That we stole? That we are thieves?"

"Bad? Amica, we did something good. All this gold, it was of no use in the ground. In our hands it's alive."

"Good or bad depends on what you use it for," Pollio said, "if you use it for something good, or if you just use it."

"But think of Green Gnaeus. He spent decades building his fortune, growing the Treasure of Juno Moneta, and in one night we took it all away from him. What is he supposed to do now?"

"Appia," Lucius said, "Green Gnaeus, he—"

"Lucius!" Flamma interrupted and yanked Lucius from behind, causing him to fall backward and hit the ground with a thump. "You know I said – lost Jadecrystal when you free me? Not. Not lost it."

"What do you mean *not*?"

Flamma waved for Brontes. The lizardwolf faithfully slithered forward. She opened her mouth. Under her tongue, a green stone sparkled.

Is that… Appia thought, and saw how Lucius turned pale.

"No, no," Lucius mumbled. "It's impossible. Impossible,

I tell you!"

"I knew you happy," Flamma said, smiling broadly.

"No, no, little half-cyclops, you don't understand. *That's* not the Jadecrystal! *That's* the stone I bought years ago, the one that made me start playing the lottery. It's not the real Jadecrystal!"

"If your stone is here," Pollio said, "then what exactly does Clemens have?"

"Hurry," Lucius cried, already at the drinking horses. "We gotta go, we gotta go now!"

Appia tried to drag Incitatus away. The unicorn hadn't finished drinking, and refused to leave the pond.

"Leave him!" Lucius ordered as no progress was made. "The horses will have to do."

"Leave him? Lucius, it's *Incitatus*."

"We don't have time!"

Appia stared into the unicorn's eyes. She'd never met an animal like him; no horse could match his strength, his determination. She sighed, dragging a horse to the chariot.

They sat down. Pollio, Kezekem, Flamma, and Brontes at the back, together with the coins, Lucius next to her in front. Appia took one last look at Incitatus, but the animal kept his head deep in the water. She gave the horses a good whirl with the whip.

They took a few dragging steps, and came to a halt.

"Oh, Dis-it! What are you doing? Whip harder!"

Appia whipped again – same result. "It's Incitatus. He's the one who pulled us. The horses can't manage without him."

They all jumped down from the chariot, making new attempts with Incitatus, but no matter how they dragged and begged the unicorn, he refused to budge. Still there was water to drink.

There was a splash as Lucius threw a sack into the water.

It instantly sank to the bottom.

"Amicus, no!" Kezekem cried. "The gold, amicus! The gold!"

"There is no other way," Lucius said bitterly. "We must reduce our weight if we are ever to get out of here."

"But amicus," Kezekem said, eyes filled with tears, "take these then." And he lifted the sacks in the chariot. There, at the bottom, were loads of bags, small but heavy.

"The Gods, Kezekem!" Lucius exclaimed. "I've told you not to bother with metal scraps!"

"I couldn't resist, amicus, I just couldn't resist. They have a value too, right? And I thought, some compensation for the sack the weeprechaun took to the bottom of the bottomless abyss, we deserve that."

They threw the bags in the pond, and climbed back into the chariot. Now, when Appia whipped the horses, they moved forward, albeit not with the same furious speed as when Incitatus had led them. They were back on the road, and it was empty of traffic.

A sharp curve was approaching.

"Odd," Appia said. "I thought the roads from Rome were all straight. That's just a little grove, how come the road goes around it and not through it?"

"It's just something you say," Lucius said through his teeth.

Appia shrugged and drove past a merchant. "How should I know?"

"Amici… have a look behind, will you?"

Behind, Appia thought, *the Praetorians!* She turned her head, but what she saw was worse than Praetorians. The road was clogged with hundreds – no, *thousands* – of travelers: pedestrians, riders, carts of all sizes.

"Hey, watch it!" A white-haired old hag lay on the

ground with a basket balanced her head, and a dozen cabbage heads around her. Some of the produce rolled away and got crushed under the traffic.

Appia slowed the horses, turning onto the route that was even more jammed than the start of a race. They had a clear line of sight once more.

There rose seven hills and an enormous city.

"By Dis Pater," Lucius whispered.

"But," Appia said, "we've been driving straight ahead. Straight ahead, right until this moment."

"The Jadecrystal," Lucius mumbled, shaking his head. "It has called us back. There is no escape. A thousand roads – they all lead to Rome. No wonder it's always so crowded."

XXIX

The world was spinning. On his way up Tarpeian Rock, Clemens had been drinking wine. Lots of wine. For Rome had a new Emperor.

Not the blemmye Valerius Asiaticus, whose immense wealth and political network were the envy of many, and whose serious manner made him more suitable than any human Clemens knew of. Not the sly and cunning Senator Annius Vinicianus, supported by his powerful uncle Marcus Vinicius. Not the Emperor's two-year-old daughter, who had her brains knocked out against a wall.

No, a slave had scrubbed blood from the palace floor, and found a limping imbecile behind a curtain who apparently was Emperor Caligula's uncle. A living relative, and no matter how forgotten the imbecile had been – no matter how he dragged his foot behind his every step – he was now known as the Emperor.

And it was all Clemens' fault.

Ma Kuang and his friends had used him in an attack on Rome, replacing a bad Emperor with a dumb one, and all Clemens got in return was a perfectly normal stone. He understood it now, finally. How could the Jadecrystal be real, how could it have the extraordinary powers the alchemist spoke of, when it hadn't protected the Emperor; when it hadn't warned

him of the conspiracy against his life, when it had let knives tear
through his body?

Clemens looked down at the world, at Rome, which
still spun in a furious manner. There, eighty-five feet below, the
ground was hard and flat. Wet too. The sky opened up like never
before. The wind tugged at his ears, and Clemens squeezed the
stone even tighter.

He took a deep breath and embraced the end.

He threw the Jadecrystal off the cliff. It glittered green
in the air, sailing through great raindrops as it fell. Then, green
shards below. Thousands of pieces, like the blood of a green
monster. It was over.

"You really shouldn't have done that."

Clemens turned around. The rain had muffled the
sound of his steps, but there he was, almost within spitting
distance, he with a wart on his forehead; he who had stolen right
under Clemens' nose. The Gladiator Thief, Lucius Turpilinus.

"The crystal," Lucius said, "it had powers. Greater than
any of us understand. Perhaps it could've saved you."

Clemens snorted, even though he hated snorting – it
made him feel like a bull. "Where are your friends?"

"Guarding the treasure. There are thieves everywhere
these days."

"I see," Clemens said, feeling his face growing
increasingly wet. The wind was hitting him directly, now. "I
killed him, by the way."

Lucius blinked. "You killed... who?"

"Thrakatulus. I stomped him to death. It probably
means war with the Vigiles, but he ruined everything. Thought
it might make you happy to hear."

Lucius shook his head. "You're sick. But you did a good
job with the Emperor, I'll give you that. What did you think of
Ma Kuang?"

Clemens felt as if he'd sunk into a swamp of icy water *and* horse dung. "Ma Kuang? What do you know of him?"

"Well – red robe, mustache, all that. The accent may have been an exaggeration, but he was a funny guy, wasn't he? He's based on a merchant who sold me a stone once."

"*You!* You're Ma Kuang!"

Lucius chuckled. "Not a good enough actor, I'm afraid. No, I believe you know him as Chymes the Alchemist."

"Chymes? Impossible. Ma Kuang doesn't have a beard, I would've recognized him. I—"

Lucius threw back his head and guffawed violently. "Did you really believe that silliness! Ha ha! A beard of kelp! Of seagrass! You're out of your mind!"

"I'll punish you," Clemens said, taking a step forward. "Finally I'll punish you for everything you've done."

Lucius made a gesture with his open palms. "No thanks, I'll pass. Fighting has never been my strong suit."

"You must! By Saturn, you must! You've tricked me from the start!"

Lucius sighed. He put his hand to his neck and drew a dark sword from his back. A spatha, one of the deadliest weapons in Rome, forged of pure black eel iron.

"The Gods, I thought you said you didn't want to fight!"

Lucius shrugged. "I had a feeling you'd insist."

Clemens rushed forward, his hooves quick on the wet cliff. He kept his head down, his horns pointed at the enemy. As Lucius jumped aside, Clemens snapped his head and hit something soft, a stomach perhaps. He heard Lucius curse, and from the corner of his eye he saw the dark sword swooping down. He threw himself backwards. The draft beat against his face.

Lucius moved sideways, Clemens followed and they circled each other like planets around the Earth. It spun before

Clemens eyes; the wine still affected him. They completed a semicircle, leaving Clemens once again at the edge of the cliff, and Lucius attacked.

Clemens ducked too slowly. Fire in his shoulder. Blood pouring out. Saturn, the sword was sharp. He screamed, but the pain wouldn't go away. Stumbling steps, almost losing his balance. Lucius was approaching, thrusting the sword through his armor and straight into the chest. Tore out the heart with the tip of the sword. Triumphant eyes.

Clemens counterattacked.

He blocked a blow with his horns, sending the sword flying down the cliff. Enemy disarmed. Punch, punch, punch. Lucius' face was soft. Everything was so damn soft with humans. His back heart pumped quicker, granting his fist power. Punch, punch, punch. Sound of broken bones. Lucius lay on the ground.

Clemens took a few wheezing breaths, trying to ignore the pain. Just a little more, then he could rest. He wanted to fling the thief down the cliff, but he couldn't. Too tired. He would end it here and now by stomping. Clemens lifted his hooves. Bloody eyes gazed up on him.

His bottom stung. He stumbled backwards. His tail! That bastard had pulled him by the tail! The world spun. Another step – and he lost his grip.

He looked up at the cliff as he fell to his death.

XXX

Lucius didn't know how long he'd been lying there. His face was hot, but the rain washed it pleasantly. Slowly, he brought his hand to his cheek, nose, mouth. He couldn't open his left eye, and he felt shattered teeth with his tongue.

Well, he thought, *at least I'll no longer be known as the guy with a wart on his forehead.*

He sat up, pushing off the dizziness. Stepped to the edge. A body lay down there, parts scattered. Clemens.

And I didn't even have the chance to tell you the best part about our alchemist friend. He's been practicing limping every night the last three months.

When Lucius walked down Capitoline Hill in search of his companions, the city was quiet. As if it mourned. Or was knocked out. Around him, the gods poured rain, but Lucius wasn't cold.

They waited at the Forum. All clearly wounded but alive. Sitting around the treasure lying in the open. The Forum was deserted now, but the bodies were so numerous that Lucius wondered if he'd truly fought the hardest battle.

Behind them loomed the Temple of Vesta; the sacred fire had died, and the Vestals themself lay dead on the ground with their snake hair hacked to pieces.

Appia rose to her feet. "Lucius, Lucius! Your face!"

Flamma nodded. "We brothers now. You, me – one-eyed gladiators."

"You got it, right?" Kezekem said. "The Jadecrystal?"

"No."

Kezekem groaned. "So we're stuck here? Amicus, you know I like you, but all this gold and nowhere to go…"

"We don't have to run," Lucius said. "Not anymore. Clemens is dead."

"There are others," Pollio remarked tiredly. "Others who'll hunt us."

Lucius shook his head. It throbbed in response. "We'll ask the new Emperor for mercy. He who limps. He'll grant it, and let us keep our treasure. That much he owes us."

"No he won't."

Lucius turned around slowly, so that his body didn't cause him more needless pain. There he was, the new Emperor. Dressed in a solid purple toga, decorated with imagery spun in gold thread; a white tunic underneath, and on his head, a magnificent laurel wreath. He wasn't even wet, as if the rain dared not to lay hands upon him.

He'd come to meet them in their triumph. Not that strange perhaps – he always had a nose for gold, that one. But what was it he'd said? "Won't?" Lucius narrowed his working eye. "No mercy?"

Chymes, the Emperor, although he probably called himself something else now – Claudius, Lucius recalled – said, "Mercy? Sure, what do I care? Some petty thieves are no harm to my Empire. But that treasure you've got there, I'll take that, thank you very much."

Lucius went cold, but had no strength left to be upset. "No. You can't. We had a deal."

Chymes raised his eyebrows, an expression that made

Lucius realize how silly the Emperor's face looked. Or rather, how perfectly normal it looked, which was so different from his previous face dominated by that massive sea-inspired beard, that it was silly in itself.

"If anyone should know that I cannot be trusted, it's you." He pointed with his thumb at the two dozen Praetorians that accompanied him, gazing hungrily at the gold. "These bodyguards aren't cheap, for starters. They didn't seem very loyal to my predecessor, so I thought they could use some extra motivation. They've been treated poorly for far too long – I even found their prefect lying in a rather uncomfortable position not far from here."

Lucius sighed. He wasn't in the mood to debate, not now, and certainly not with someone like Chymes. "Look around. You think all these bodies fell from the sky? That these Vestals here stumbled head first into a bunch of knives? We've already fought hard for our treasure. We won't let some fake-dimwit, fake-Emperor take it away from us."

As he spoke, Lucius felt his strength return through the support of his friends. Maybe he was in the mood for a debate, after all. Flamma beat his chest, Brontes hissed, Pollio tried and failed miserably to look menacing, Appia raised her whip, and Kezekem did some weird shit with his foot.

"Yeah," the sciapod added, "and you can stuff your mercy in a sack, non-amicus!"

"No, no," Lucius shushed him, "we still want that. Mercy *and* treasure, that's what we want."

"Oh, er… in a *great* sack! And give the sack to us, so it's mercy, right? To us. And we keep the real sacks, the treasure sacks."

The Emperor raised his eyebrows again. "Petty thieves, indeed. That's it, I'm taking the treasure." He snapped his fingers, making the Praetorians approach with drawn swords.

The advance halted, however, as Flamma came to meet them. "No taking treasure! Treasure ours!"

Lucius looked at the Praetorians scrambling up a defense formation to face the half-cyclops. There were more than twenty of the goatmen, but the odds weren't exactly in their favor. Flamma was held back by nothing this time; it would be a massacre.

The Emperor raised his hand. "Before you sic your brute on me, ask yourself if he's big enough to defeat all of Rome? For that is what you must do if you wish to keep your treasure. Only the Emperor is that big."

Empty words, Lucius thought, but with an eerie feeling in his bones. If it was one thing he knew about Chymes – even if this Emperor role made him speak and act so differently – it was that he *never* took a risk. Not when gold was involved.

Chymes smiled, as if he'd read Lucius' mind. "Did you really think I only brought two dozen Praetorians for a mission like this? It took some time to organize them, sure, but they should be here any moment now."

As if on signal – and they probably were, perhaps by that hand Chymes had raised – several hundred Praetorians, an entire cohort, came marching toward them in the rain. Clad in armor, and carrying a standard in the shape of a silver *aquila* with stretched wings. They were ready for war.

"Behold," Chymes proclaimed in a manner that was painfully theatrical to Lucius' ears, "the power of being Emperor!" The army arrived, crowding on the Forum and on the streets behind.

"You're Emperor because of me," Lucius said, spitting blood from his fight on Tarpeian Rock. "Because of us."

Chymes made a dismissive gesture. "Like I said, being Emperor brings a lot of expenses. And someone once told me that the best way to make gold is simply by taking someone else's."

Very funny, Lucius thought, knowing it was over. That they'd lost. There was no fighting an army.

"You're not gonna bite them, are you?" he muttered as Chymes embraced one of the sacks in a very un-imperial manner. Lucius had grown quite fond of his coins the short time he'd had them in his possession, and preferred not to see them end up in the mouth of a man with such an infamous lack of dental hygiene.

There was no answer to this remark, and shortly thereafter, there was nothing left at the Forum except a crew of thieves in the rain.

"Well," Lucius said, wet to his very bones, "that's one way to pay a debt."

"Tell me about it," Kezekem said, shaking with anger in a way that must've been very unpleasant for the flea population inhabiting his face. "Nineteen quadrans, amicus! That rat still owes me *nineteen quadrans* and didn't say a word!"

Pollio, apparently somehow blessed by not yet fully grasping the infirmity of Kezekem's mind, said, "Nineteen quadrans? What about the seven hundred sixty-three thousand denarii he just took from us?"

"Eh, amicus, you win some, you lose some. 'Tis part of the game. But those nineteen quadrans, there're mine I tell you!"

"Actually," Lucius said, realizing the poor timing but hardly able to pass up on the opportunity to correct some numbers, "it's more like seven hundred *forty-seven* thousand denarii; since Green Gnaeus took a sack to the bottom of the abyss, and we threw another into that pond."

As soon as his words left his mouth, all of them had the exact same idea. Pollio was the first to say it. "The pond! We got eight thousand denarii waiting for us in that pond."

"And Incitatus might still be there," Appia added. "I'm

sure he's eager to race at the Circus again. But with a new driver this time."

"Yeah amici," Kezekem said, waving his foot with such intensity that the mixture of water and sweat flying from it would've been highly unpleasant to his surroundings, had it not been for the fact that it was already raining, "and we got some real good metal scraps in that water too. Worth a fortune I tell you!"

"Ah yes, Kez," Flamma said. "You take scraps – we take coins. Ha!"

They looked at Lucius – as if it were a play where everyone on stage were to say something – and Lucius in turn looked at Brontes, who'd seemingly been highly involved in defending the treasure when it still had been theirs to defend. The bodies around her were burned, creatures of all kinds blinded by the treasure and in an attempt to become thieves turned into ashes. The lizardwolf was shining from within, leaking light through her scales. Half lizard, half wolf... and half thunderbolts?

"There's been a lot of talk about debts," Lucius said, "but it seems I've forgotten the most important one. You go to the pond. This is enough for me." He stuck his hand into Brontes' mouth, dug into the mucus behind her tongue and pulled out the stone. It was ice-cold. "Maybe jade can heal a tree."

ABOUT THE AUTHOR

Addicted to history, Axel spends his days reading documents from lost times. Not only does this make him curse at unreadable eighteenth-century handwriting, but also lets him shamelessly steal ideas from widely different eras for his writing projects. A fantasy freak since a young age, he lives in Sweden with his two sharp-clawed, long-tailed dragons (sometimes referred to as "cats").

For more information about Axel, please visit his website at **axelkamne.com.**

ACKNOWLEDGMENTS

I'd like to thank everyone at 8th & Atlas Publishing for making this book possible. A big thank you to my editor Christina De Paris, who has provided feedback and encouragement throughout, and was especially helpful in the translation process.

Thank you to everyone in my writing group, who have written with me, given me feedback, and most importantly *fikat*. Thank you to those who have helped me in writing courses and elsewhere.

Finally, I'd like to thank everyone on planet Earth, except those who don't deserve it.